JACK STAPLES
AND THE RING *of* TIME

JACK STAPLES

AND THE RING *of* TIME

MARK BATTERSON
and
JOEL N. CLARK

David C Cook®
transforming lives together

JACK STAPLES AND THE RING OF TIME
Published by David C Cook
4050 Lee Vance View
Colorado Springs, CO 80918 U.S.A.

David C Cook Distribution Canada
55 Woodslee Avenue, Paris, Ontario, Canada N3L 3E5

David C Cook U.K., Kingsway Communications
Eastbourne, East Sussex BN23 6NT, England

The graphic circle C logo is a registered trademark of David C Cook.

This story is a work of fiction. All characters and events are the product of the author's
imagination. Any resemblance to any person, living or dead, is coincidental.

LCCN 2014943142
ISBN 978-0-7814-1107-3
eISBN 978-1-4347-0861-8

© 2014 Mark Batterson, Joel N. Clark
Published in association with the literary agency of The Fedd
Agency, Inc., Post Office Box 341973, Austin, Texas 78734.

The Team: Alex Field, Jamie Chavez, Carly Razo, Nick Lee, Karen Athen
Cover Design: Amy Konyndyk
Cover Illustration: Duncan Stewart

Printed in the United States of America
First Edition 2014

1 2 3 4 5 6 7 8 9 10

063014

Chapter 1

A NIGHT TO REMEMBER

A blackbird fluttered through the open flap of an enormous circus tent. Only one boy out of the hundreds of men, women, and children sitting inside noticed. The boy was as thin as a rail with bushy brown hair and bright blue eyes. His name was Jack Staples, and today was his eleventh birthday. Jack sat sandwiched between his fourteen-year-old brother, Parker, and his mother, whose age he did not know.

No one else in the crowd had noticed the bird because their attention was drawn to the center of the tent where a girl in a crimson hooded cloak walked along a rope suspended between two platforms. The girl's daring walk was only part of what had the onlookers so entranced. Not far beneath her tightrope, two lions—one with a golden mane, the other's black—circled and snarled. As the girl walked the rope, the beasts leaped and swiped their razor-sharp claws, barely missing her feet. With each miss, they roared their frustration, and the crowd gasped in fear.

Encircling the lions was a blazing ring of fire. And just outside the flames were four tumblers. Each held a torch and moved continuously, somersaulting and leaping about to ensure the beasts stayed within the circle of flames and away from the watching crowd.

Jack should have been mesmerized by the death-defying spectacle, yet he was becoming more irritated by the second. As the balancing girl neared the center of the rope, bringing the bottoms of her feet closer to the lions' claws with every step, Jack couldn't stop his eyes from drifting upward. The annoying blackbird was still flapping about near the tent ceiling.

This girl, thought Jack, *is only moments away from being eaten, and here I am looking at a stupid bird!*

Jack's eyes shot downward as the crowd gasped. The girl flailed her arms, trying to regain her balance. Jack clutched his brother's hand as the rope pitched and swayed beneath her.

Throughout the tent, the crowd shouted instructions and words of encouragement. Just as it seemed the girl was sure to plunge to her death, she stretched out her right leg and stood on the toes of her left foot. Amazingly, these movements allowed her to regain balance.

A collective sigh of relief rose from the stands as the balancing girl took the final step to the center of the rope. The beasts bounded upward, gnashed their teeth, and roared wildly. Outside the flames the tumblers flipped and spun as their blurred torches sent sparks hurling in every direction. Jack didn't breathe. Even when something hard and cold bumped against his leg from beneath the bleachers, he barely noticed.

As the tightrope walker crouched low, she wrapped her crimson cloak around her body. At the same moment, the tumblers gave a final leap before also dropping to their knees.

The black-maned lion roared as both beasts bounded upward, snapping their jaws at the girl taunting them from above. Yet the girl also leaped high, spreading her crimson cloak wide and performing the most magnificent spinning backflip.

As she landed, the rope pitched dangerously beneath her, but she maintained her balance. And when she extended her arms wide, the crimson cloak enveloped each, making her look like a bird with wings outstretched. From beneath her hood, the girl grinned widely.

For a moment, perfect silence hung inside the circus tent. Even the stupid bird was quiet. And then, as if it were the easiest thing in the world, the tightrope walker stood tall and bowed, giving an extravagant flourish of her cloak.

The crowd roared their praise; Jack let out a great sigh of relief. When the poised girl turned to continue up the rope to the opposite platform, she made it look as if the rope were as wide as a road and she didn't have a care in the world. The applause grew to a crescendo as men threw hats and children high into the air.

"I was so scared!" Jack had to yell to be heard above the cheers of the crowd.

"Me too!" shouted Parker. "Did you see how close those claws came?" Parker made a growling sound and curled his hand into a claw, mimicking the lions.

Jack laughed as his eyes drifted to the ceiling once more. The blackbird was still flapping about and screeching loudly. As the girl continued her walk to safety, the ridiculous bird rammed into the ceiling one final time and then plummeted downward in a daze.

Crouched low on the sandy ground was the black-maned lion. Its eyes were also locked on the falling bird. With a new target in sight, the beast leaped higher than ever before. And though it missed the bird, it did manage to chomp through the tightrope.

Shrill screams erupted as the lion landed on the sandy ground. Fingers pointed toward the dazed girl who was now lying between the two beasts. The lions seemed puzzled at the girl's presence, yet it was only when the four tumblers leaped into the ring of fire that the beasts became angry.

The tumblers stood shoulder-to-shoulder, shouting as they whirled their torches with dizzying speed, thrusting them forward in a threatening manner. But the lions stood their ground. No matter how close the men came, the beasts refused to back away from the girl. They paced in front of her, roaring at the approaching men.

The tumblers were now so close to the lions that they could have touched the beasts with their firebrands. Yet the lions swiped at the torches, refusing to move. As the men took yet another step forward, both lions let out a defiant roar, then turned and took three running steps toward the now unguarded ring of fire … and jumped.

The crowd surged into motion, people screaming and running wildly in every direction. The lions' roars were like thunder as they bounded into the mass of men, women, and children, nipping and swiping at anyone unfortunate enough to be in their way.

Jack was terrified. His mother grabbed his hand, as well as Parker's, and began running toward the exit. Even without the lions, though, the run was perilous. The crowd had become frantic. Everyone sprinted blindly with no regard for those around them. It was chaos.

Jack's mother skidded to a stop, knelt, and pulled both boys close. As the panicked crowd sprinted past, Jack could see where she was looking. On the far side of the tent, a young girl sat on the sandy ground, screaming. A short distance away, the golden lion stalked slowly toward the girl.

Jack's mother placed Parker's hand over his. "Parker," she shouted, "take your brother and get him out of here. I need to go help that girl." As the crowd rushed past, bumping and jostling them without care, Jack's mother bent and kissed each of them on the forehead. "Make your way to the wagon, and I'll meet you there as soon as I can." Without another word, she gently shoved them in the direction of the exit, then turned and ran back for the girl.

Jack was panicked. Parker dragged him a few steps toward the exit, but Jack escaped his brother's grasp and ran backward, desperate to find his mother in the crowd. *What is she doing?* he wondered. *She's going to be eaten by the lion!*

Parker caught up to Jack and tugged his arm, shouting, "We have to keep running!" Jack hadn't realized he'd stopped. When he turned to continue his run, the fabric walls of the circus tent burst into flames. Someone must have knocked over one of the lampstands, he realized. Both boys shared a fearful look as the fire spread quicker than Jack could have imagined. They bolted forward again as the flames shot toward the ceiling and thick smoke filled the air.

Jack struggled to keep his feet as Parker was knocked to his knees only to get up again and continue running. Jack looked over his shoulder one last time in hopes of finding his mother, but she was lost amid the smoke and hysteria. As he turned back, he collided headfirst with someone's elbow. Bouncing backward, Jack landed flat on his back on the sandy ground.

For a moment, everything went dark. Then, as his vision returned, he felt disoriented. He stared at the ceiling in a daze. It was positively beautiful. Bright flames danced far above as bits of fire and ash fell all around. He lay on his back watching in wonder, the flaming walls and ceiling seemingly spinning around him.

"Jack!" Someone's scream interrupted his cloudy thoughts. "You put me down! Jack! Can you hear me?" the voice screamed again.

Why are the walls on fire? And why does my head hurt? Jack's mind felt sluggish.

"Jack! Get up! I'm telling you, put me down!" The same voice shouted again, yet this time it sounded farther away.

I recognize that voice. That's Parker! As he sat up to look for his brother, tears leaked from his eyes. The air was filled with billowing smoke that was growing thicker by the second.

"You let me go! That's my brother in there! Let me go!"

Jack finally saw him; Parker was in the arms of a large man who was carrying him away like a sack of grain. His brother hit the man with his fists and continued yelling to Jack.

"Get up, Jack! It's coming! You have to get up! The lion is coming!"

Before Parker could say more, the man had carried him out of the tent.

As fire exploded along the cloth walls, Jack remembered where he was. And with the memory came a paralyzing fear.

Chapter 2

WITHIN THE FLAMES

The blazing ceiling sent ash and embers floating down in an other-worldly rainfall, yet Jack Staples didn't move a muscle. Utterly terrified, he sat alone on the hot, sandy ground in the center of the burning circus tent. The heat was blistering, the air shimmered, and the fire danced, yet Jack could not make himself stand.

Suddenly, from somewhere deep within the flames came a voice that rasped with the sound of a freshly dug grave.

"COME TO ME," it creaked. "YOU CANNOT HIDE FOREVER."

The fire was so hot Jack was sure his skin would soon burst into flames. However, the voice was far more terrifying than mere fire ever could be. Once again it called to him.

"YOU WILL NOT ESCAPE ME," it rasped. "TOGETHER, WE WILL DESTROY THE AWAKENED AND RULE THIS WORLD. THE PROPHECY DEMANDS IT. YOU ARE MINE!"

As Jack lifted his arms to shield himself from the voice, he thought he saw a bright and horrible … something, standing in the midst of the inferno. Yet when he looked again, there was nothing but raging fire.

But then Jack saw the shadow of a great beast reflected in the smoke, approaching from the opposite direction. Fear gripped him as the shadow quickly resolved into one of the circus lions. The beast looked otherworldly striding through the thick veil of ash and smoke.

Large firebrands cascaded from the walls and ceiling, yet Jack couldn't make himself move. Without slowing, the mighty lion stalked straight up to him and let out a fierce growl. It was the lion with the golden mane, and as it looked at Jack, its eyes reflected the light of the burning flames.

Firebrands landed all around, and the smoke grew steadily thicker, but neither beast nor boy took notice. Both stared at each other as if in a trance. Ever so slowly, Jack stood. Tears streamed from his smoke-filled eyes, and his skin burned, but he didn't look away. Without thinking, he reached out and touched the beast's shoulder, tracing his finger along the length of a small scar. And as he touched the mighty lion, it began to purr.

For a long moment, Jack and the lion were completely still. Smoldering fragments rained down while flames hissed and danced.

Finally, the beast let out a small sigh and glanced at the burning tent. Jack also looked. The blazing walls were both beautiful and terrifying.

As Jack began to cough from the thick smoke filling his lungs, the great beast nudged him with its nose and then inhaled deeply. Without warning the lion let out a thunderous roar. The roar was so powerful that the force of it knocked Jack flat on his back.

Lying on blistering sand surrounded by a raging fire, Jack was sure he was about to die.

Outside the tent, the world was chaos. Full night had fallen, and in the minutes after the fire erupted, a massive thundercloud broke overhead. Rain poured down, and lightning streaked the sky. The dirt roads were quickly churned into mud as beast and human ran frantically in every direction.

Parker stood in the midst of it, in the pouring rain, his eyes fixed on the burning tent. The same man who'd carried him out of the tent stood just behind, holding him firmly by the shoulders.

"I'm letting go of you now, but you need to promise you won't try to go back in there again," the man said gruffly.

"I could have saved him," Parker cried. "I told you to put me down. I could have saved him!"

"Boy, if I hadn't grabbed you when I did, you'd be as dead as he is. There was nothing you could have done." The man pointed his finger at Parker. "I need to go now. Don't do anything stupid." Without another word he walked away.

A beastly roar came from somewhere deep inside the burning tent, and as it sounded, Parker collapsed to his knees and wept.

A short distance away, a tusked elephant ran past as men and women dove into the mud to get out of its way. An arctic wolf trotted in the opposite direction, followed by an ape that seemed to be chasing an ostrich. Yet Parker barely noticed any of it. His attention was on the flames stretching into the night sky.

"Parker! Jack! Where are you?"

Parker stood slowly.

"Parker! Jack! Do you hear me?"

It was his mother's voice. She was alive! He wanted to call out to her, but how could he? Jack was dead because of him. Just as he was about to turn away, his mother caught his eye.

"Parker! Son, I've been calling you. Didn't you hear me?" She ran over and threw her arms around him. "I am so glad you're safe. I was worried about you." After a moment, she froze. Keeping her hands on his shoulders, she leaned back.

"Where is your brother?" Her voice was quiet, though it still held the sound of alarm.

Parker opened his mouth, but no sound came. His mother's face shifted from alarm to horror as she dropped to her knees. Rain continued to pour down, and lightning streaked the night sky. Wild and exotic animals galloped and pranced all around, yet neither Parker nor his mother paid them any attention. Both just stared into the flames.

After a long moment, his mother stood and placed a hand on his shoulder. "Your brother is not dead," she said, wiping tears from her eyes. "I will not believe it, and you mustn't either. He is the Child of Prophecy. And he will lead the Awakened in the Last Battle. I do not believe this fire will kill him."

Parker knew his brother was special. But as he watched the blistering flames rocket into the night sky, he couldn't make himself believe Jack was still alive. He didn't think anyone could survive that. Not even the Child of Prophecy.

It took four hours for the larger flames to burn out, and the sun had not yet risen when Parker's mother walked into the ashes. Red-hot embers covered the ground while small flames danced throughout. As the rain subsided, every drop sent smoke billowing upward. Silhouetted by smoke and flames, Parker's mother continued forward until the haze obscured her completely.

Minutes passed. Parker began to fear for his mother's safety. He stood, nervously wondering if he should follow her in.

"Parker! I need you," she called, her voice muted by the heavy haze. "Come, my boy!"

Parker darted forward, hope blooming in his chest. His feet warmed as the soles of his shoes began to burn. When he found his mother at the center of the burned-out tent, she was kneeling before a mass of matted fur and seared flesh.

It's the lion, Parker realized as hope dissolved into fear. He didn't want to find his brother's body if it was going to look anything like this poor beast. "Mother, what are you doing?" he cried.

"Get down here and help me push!" she said through teary eyes. "It's too heavy, and I need your help."

The body of the lion shifted ever so slightly.

What? Parker couldn't believe it. Unsure what was happening, he did as his mother asked. Kneeling on hot ashes, Parker and his mother shoved the beast with all their might. And there, lying unconscious on the sandy ground and looking as if he'd been in the sun for days, was Jack Staples.

The searing light brought an agony that cut to the bone.

"I love you, my boy," Jack's mother whispered. "You are safe with me now."

Jack opened his eyes as pain coursed through his body. He was lying in a wagon bed with his head in his mother's lap. Parker sat up front, driving.

"Where …," Jack croaked. He stopped and tried to work moisture into his mouth. "Where are we?" he rasped.

"We are almost home. We left the circus this morning, and we will be home within the hour."

As he looked up at his mother, he blinked. A strange light was glowing from somewhere deep in her chest. *I must be imagining things*, he thought. Yet even as he watched, her hands moved in a strange pattern as they gathered the light. Smiling at him, she touched his burning skin, and where she touched, the pain began to subside.

"We will be home soon, I promise."

Far too exhausted to keep his eyes open a moment longer, Jack fell fast asleep.

Chapter 3

THE SHADOWFOG

The morning after they arrived home from the circus fire, Jack's brother and father left Ballylesson to make a delivery of stone and mortar to a nearby village. His father worked as a stonemason, and both boys often worked alongside him. A few days later, his father and Parker were still gone and had sent word to Jack and his mother that they wouldn't be back for another week at least.

Jack quickly learned that he had become a bit of a legend in Ballylesson. Everyone wanted to hear the story of the boy who'd been saved by the lion. Yet he hated talking about it; he didn't even like thinking about it. Everything about that night at the circus confused him. Why would a lion sacrifice itself to save him?

Five days after the fire, Jack felt much better. Doctor Falvey called his recovery "a miracle." He said it should have taken weeks for the burns to heal, yet within a few short days, they were almost gone.

Around three in the afternoon, on a cloudy Thursday, Jack was feeling desperate to leave the house. He'd been stuck in bed for a few days. Earlier in the week his best friend, Arthur Greaves, had come to visit, and the boys had promised to meet in the woods outside the schoolhouse on Thursday afternoon.

Jumping down the stairs four at a time and running into the kitchen, Jack called out, "Mother, can I go and meet Arthur?"

"I don't know," his mother answered. "Doctor Falvey said you need to take it easy. How are you feeling?"

"Really good, Mother. I promise. Please, may I go? I haven't been outside in ages!"

She paused a moment, then smiled. "I guess I'm going to have to let you fly free at some point. But promise me you won't be running about too much. I don't want you to lose your breath."

"Yes, Mother." Jack grinned and immediately darted for the front door.

"If it starts to rain," she called after him, "you come straight home!"

"Yes, Mother!" he yelled over his shoulder.

Jack ran straight into the woods. A week before the circus fire, Jack, Parker, and Arthur had begun building what Jack believed would one day become a mighty fortress. At the moment it was only a piece of wood wedged between two branches high up in a tree, but they had plans to add more boards in the coming days.

As he arrived at the widest and tallest oak in the forest, Jack immediately began to climb. When he was nearly halfway up, something inexplicable happened. The air felt different—sharper somehow. Before he could think about what had changed, a mighty wind ripped through the forest, shaking the surrounding trees and sending earth and leaves flying. As the wind passed over Jack, he was petrified. His fingers gripped the branch above while his feet stayed rooted to the branch below.

Then the wind passed, and something else changed. The forest was absolutely silent. It wasn't the silence of nothing happening, as when wind blows through leaves, birds sing their songs, and crickets chirp. It was as if time itself were holding its breath.

As he held tightly to the tree, Jack heard the sound of a thousand voices whispering in his ear.

"I SSSSEE YOU," the voices rasped.

Jack leaped back without thinking. Only when he was falling through the air did he realize his mistake. As he dropped toward the forest floor, he heard the ringing of bells somewhere in the distance.

When he opened his eyes, Jack gasped for breath. He was in his house, lying in the center of the upstairs hallway and feeling as if someone had punched him in the stomach. From somewhere in the distance, he could still hear the ringing of bells; though, as he listened, they quickly faded. He searched his mind, trying to remember what he had just been doing, but nothing came to him.

Standing on shaky legs, he breathed in deeply, trying to fill his lungs. When he opened the door to his bedroom, the only light came from the full moon shining through the window.

Jack was surprised to find his mother standing by the window and looking out. Next to her was a golden-haired girl a little taller than Jack.

"How can you ask this of me, Elion?" Jack's mother said.

The girl, Jack supposed her name was Elion, spoke. "And you think you can keep her safe from what's coming? You think you can stop him?" Elion's voice had a strange musical quality.

Jack's mother began to cry. "But this is my child; she is mine!"

As his mother turned to face Elion, Jack saw her cradling a baby in her arms.

Elion reached up and placed a comforting hand on his mother's shoulder. "This is the Child of Prophecy, and you know as well as I that he is coming. If I don't take her now, all will be lost." She turned to look at the cloudless sky. "We are not the only ones who can read the stars. The Lion's Eye has been opened."

"Mother, what's going on?" Jack interrupted.

Both Elion and his mother spun around, his mother shielding the baby with her body and Elion drawing a short sword from inside her cloak. Elion stood on the tips of her toes, assuming a very dangerous-looking stance.

"Who are you, boy?" Elion demanded. "Speak now, or die!" Her eyes seemed to gather the light of the room and shifted from deep blue to stormy gray. Jack was surprised to see that she was not a girl but a—he wasn't sure what she was. Her ears were slightly pointed, and her pale skin sparkled in the moonlight. She was unlike anyone Jack had ever seen and was absolutely beautiful.

Jack turned to his mother. "Mother, it's me, Jack! What's going on?"

His mother looked at him as if she'd never seen him before.

"Look at his eyes!" Elion gasped, stepping closer.

"What do you mean?" his mother demanded.

"Come here, boy." Elion lowered her sword and offered Jack her hand.

He stepped forward, feeling as if he were in a dream. Both Elion and his mother peered into his eyes.

"I don't understand," his mother whispered, taking a fearful step back. "What does it mean?" She shared a confused look with Elion as the ringing of bells rose once again and an impossibly bright light exploded in the room.

Jack gasped as his eyes shot open. For a long moment he didn't move; he just stared up at the sky, listening to the ringing of bells. He was lying on the forest floor, utterly confused. *What a strange dream*, he thought as the bells faded. *Of course my mother knows who I am.*

He rolled onto his side, and his breath caught. Not far off, thousands of thin, shadowy wisps were ascending from the forest floor. Still struggling to breathe, he rubbed his eyes, hoping to clear them.

Yet the dark tendrils were still there and growing thicker by the second. What was just as strange was that Jack was sure he could hear a whispering voice coming from somewhere deep within the dark fog, though he couldn't understand the words.

It's not just one voice, he realized. *It is hundreds of them—thousands, maybe.*

The hovering darkness was no longer just rising from the ground but was beginning to move. And the wisps weren't moving randomly or being blown by a breeze; they swayed back and forth as if searching for something.

Jack's breathing quickened as he sat up. He needed to move. He had no idea what this darkness was, but he was sure he didn't want it to touch him.

The shadowy coils began merging together, gathering into larger, finger-sized tentacles. And as the mist thickened, the whispering voices grew louder and angrier. Jack still couldn't understand them—if in fact they were saying anything—but their sound sent a chill down his spine.

After scrambling to his feet, he took a few steps back. The dark fog was spread out in front of him as far as he could see. The shadowed tendrils had become wrist-thick and were growing ever larger.

Jack had once seen old Farmer McCauley's hounds hunt a rabbit. The dogs had run back and forth, searching for the hare's scent. Once they'd smelled their prey, they had howled excitedly and bolted in the direction it had fled. As Jack watched the snaking, fist-sized tentacles, they reminded him of those hounds. The closer they came, the quicker they moved. The whispers were growing too—thousands of voices quickly resolving into a deafening roar.

As Jack stumbled back, it was clear the slithering darkness had caught his scent, and just like Farmer McCauley's hounds, it no longer swayed lazily but surged forward.

Jack let out a terrified scream as he sprinted through the forest. Behind him the tens of thousands of whispers joined together, uniting in one bone-chilling voice.

"THE CHILD," the voices boomed.

"HE IS HERE," they screamed.

"WE MUST TAKE HIM!" they thundered.

The fear that only seconds earlier had paralyzed Jack now gave him wings. Jack ran faster and harder than he'd ever run. The tentacles had become as thick as his body and were still merging together, blanketing the forest floor in an ocean of darkness. The ocean writhed and rolled as black waves rose high, crashing down behind him. And within the waves were the shapes of monstrous beings.

"THE ASSASSIN COMES," the voices roared.

"THE CHILD MUST BOW!" they shrieked.

The fog was only a few paces behind him now, rushing in on either side and threatening to crash over him. In front of Jack was a small hill, and just a little farther was the field that surrounded his school. He was desperate to find anyone who might help him wake from this nightmare. Maybe his best friend, Arthur Greaves, would still be there? He quickly looked back to see the fog closing in, and in that moment, he tripped over something large and soft. As he hit the ground, the wave of darkness crashed over him, covering Jack with its embrace.

Chapter 4

BULLIES IN TRAINING

Two years and twenty-one days earlier

At the age of nine, Arthur Greaves was slightly rounder than the other boys his age. When he mentioned this to his parents, his father laughed and told him, "It's just baby fat, my boy; it'll go away soon." But Arthur wasn't so sure.

He had only just moved to Ballylesson, which was a seven-hour's ride from where he used to live in Droylldom. He arrived early for his first day of school so he could be sure to introduce himself to his new teacher, Mrs. Dumphry. Though he'd only been in Ballylesson a few days, he'd already heard at least twenty stories about her.

"She's the oldest woman in Ireland," a neighbor boy told him.

"She's traveled to every country," the boy's older sister said.

Another day Arthur had met a boy at the butcher shop. "She's the oldest woman in the world," the boy said, though Arthur wasn't sure the boy could be trusted because he was at least two years younger.

The morning Arthur walked into the schoolhouse, he didn't know what to expect. It was pouring rain, and he was soaked when he finally made it inside. From the moment he walked in, he forgot all about Mrs. Dumphry. The schoolhouse was enormous—much bigger than his previous school. His jaw dropped at the number of chairs.

Sixteen students in one school! He'd never dreamed of a school so big. His last school in Droylldom had only five students. As he walked farther in, Arthur spotted Mrs. Dumphry—at least he thought it was her.

An old woman sat in a rocking chair facing the window. Her hair was wiry and gray and held at the back of her head in a large bun. He guessed that if she were to let it down, it would nearly touch the floor.

Arthur walked cautiously to the side of the rocking chair. His parents had taught him not to sneak up on people, especially if they were old, and Mrs. Dumphry was definitely the oldest woman he'd ever seen. Her eyes were sunken deep into her face, and her hands were so wrinkled he couldn't tell the wrinkles apart from the knuckles.

At first Arthur thought she was sleeping. Her head was bent to her chest, and her knobby hands rested on the armrests. Yet as he watched, he was horrified to see that she was completely unmoving.

She's not breathing, he thought with alarm. "Oh no," he whispered, wondering if the old woman was dead.

He coughed, partially to be polite, partially out of fear. "Hello, ma'am. My name is Arthur Greaves, and today is my first day at your school," he said. When he finished, he stood very still and watched for any sign of life.

Arthur stepped closer and spoke a little louder. "It is very good to be here. My family moved recently from Droylldom, and I am pleased to meet you." The last word came out in a squeak of fear. Arthur was sure of it—Mrs. Dumphry wasn't breathing.

He had never seen a dead person before, but he supposed if someone were to die of old age, it would be this woman. Taking one more fearful step forward, he decided to touch the poor woman on the shoulder, just to be sure. He reached out with one finger extended and shaking terribly.

"Mrs. Dumphry," Arthur whispered fearfully. "Are you …" Bringing his face close to hers, he searched for any sign of life. "Are you …"

As his finger touched her shoulder, Mrs. Dumphry's hand darted out and grabbed Arthur by the arm.

"Boo!" she said with a grin.

Arthur screamed and tried to run, but she held him in an iron grip. She leaned in, bringing her face close to his. "I'll get you, Arthur Greaves. I'll get you yet!"

Arthur was as pale as a freshly painted white fence. His heart was in his throat, and he couldn't move a muscle. Mrs. Dumphry burst into uncontrollable laughter, slapping her knee, then holding her stomach to keep from laughing too hard.

"Gets 'em every time!" she cackled. "Every time."

She stood and walked to the blackboard. After grabbing a piece of chalk, she wrote out the words *Mrs. Dumphry*.

"My name is Mrs. Dumphry," she said in a voice that was surprisingly youthful. "I have been teaching here for longer than you can imagine, and I will be teaching here when your children's children are old enough to go to school."

Arthur hadn't moved, and no color had returned to his cheeks.

"The lesson you just learned is of the utmost importance. You must never judge a scroll by its parchment," she said with a look of glee. "I can hold my breath for five minutes and still run faster than any woman I know." Mrs. Dumphry's eyes glowed with a fierce pride. "And though I am old, I am young in here"—she pointed to her head—"and in here"—she thumped her chest over her heart.

As Mrs. Dumphry danced a little jig, Arthur sat down at an empty desk, thankful he hadn't peed his pants.

A few minutes later the rest of the students began to arrive. Arthur had been assigned the only empty seat in the classroom. It was at the very back, and it took him only a minute to realize why the seat had remained empty. A cruel boy named Jonty Dobson sat next to him, and from the moment he sat down, Jonty started teasing Arthur and calling him all sorts of names.

"Hey, little piggy, who let you out of your pen?" Jonty whispered.

Arthur opened his mouth to speak but couldn't think of anything to say.

"Oinker! I don't know if we've been properly introduced," Jonty whispered. "You can call me the big, bad wolf." Jonty's grin had wickedness in it.

When Arthur finally spoke, his voice was shaking. "I'm not little piggy. My name is Arthur Greaves."

"You are a little piggy!" Jonty said. "And I am going to have fun with you this year."

"My father tells me that I am not actually fat, you know. He says it is just that some of my baby fat is refusing to go away."

Jonty's eyes widened in surprise as a great guffaw of laughter erupted. "Baby fat! That's the funniest thing I've ever heard!"

"Jonty Dobson!" Mrs. Dumphry's voice was stern. "You are worse than your father's father was. You will stay after class for a one-hour detention."

Jonty looked properly scolded as he lowered his eyes. "Yes, ma'am," he stammered, but the look he gave Arthur was one of pure murder.

When it was time for recess, Arthur stood and quickly walked out to the yard. He very deliberately did not look at Jonty. Although it was no longer raining, thick pools of mud covered the school-yard. Once outside, Arthur began looking for anyone who might be willing to talk to him. Yet wherever he looked, no one seemed the slightest bit interested.

He decided he had better walk back inside and stay near Mrs. Dumphry. He knew it would be a bad idea to meet Jonty out in the yard. Yet just as he was about to enter the schoolhouse, out walked Jonty Dobson.

"Where are you going, little piggy?" he chided. "I don't remember saying you could leave."

Arthur stumbled back. "I'm sorry. I-I didn't mean to get you in trouble," he stammered. "I'll tell Mrs. Dumphry it was my fault,

I'll tell her—" Before he could say another word, Jonty shoved him hard.

Arthur fell flat on his back and disappeared completely into the middle of a large puddle of mud. When he sat up, murky water cascaded off him. Jonty laughed so hard that he fell to his knees and began hitting the ground with his fist. "Little piggy is taking a mud bath!" he squealed, sounding somewhat like a pig himself.

Horrified, Arthur looked around to see all of the other children watching, and some were even laughing. As he began to cry, Jonty rolled on the muddy ground, laughing all the harder.

"That's not funny," said a slim boy who had thick, bushy hair and was holding a large book to his chest. "You shouldn't push people or make fun of them like that."

Arthur couldn't believe it. This boy didn't even know his name, yet here he was, standing up to Jonty Dobson, the meanest bully Arthur had ever met. The schoolyard quieted as everyone turned to watch. Even Jonty stopped laughing as he stood and faced the boy.

"What do you care? Is little piggy your girlfriend or something?" Jonty was a head taller than the slim boy with the book.

"I just think it's not very nice, that's all." The boy took a wary step back.

Behind Jonty, Arthur was trying to stand while wiping the mud from his face. Offering a wicked smile, Jonty turned, set his foot against Arthur's backside, and kicked, sending him into the mud yet again—this time flat on his face.

"Aye, little piggy, I don't remember saying you could get up."

Just then a large book slammed into Jonty's back. The slim boy had charged the bully and whacked him with his book. Unfortunately for the boy, he wasn't nearly as strong as Jonty, who was at least two years older. Without a second thought, Jonty punched the boy hard in the stomach and threw him on top of Arthur.

"Look at that! Little piggy does have a girlfriend!" Jonty snorted. A few of the boys laughed, although most just watched nervously, hoping he wouldn't pick on them next. Without another word Jonty turned and walked away with a trail of young bullies-in-training at his heels.

The slim boy groaned as he crawled off of Arthur and wiped the mud from his eyes. Arthur sat and again spit out a mouthful of mud. The boy quickly grabbed his book from the puddle and tried to wipe the mud off of the cover, which only made it muddier. After a moment, he sighed, set the book on his lap, and stuck out his hand.

"I'm Jack Staples. I'm assuming your name's not 'little piggy'?"

Two years and twenty-one days later

"Children! Come inside, and don't dally. A dallier today, a sluggard tomorrow," Mrs. Dumphry said as she marched inside the schoolhouse.

Although he still thought Mrs. Dumphry far too old to be alive, Arthur was constantly impressed by how quickly she moved. She was a living legend. No one knew her age, but she had taught in this schoolhouse for as long as anyone in town could remember.

Today had been a good day for Arthur so far. The good days just so happened to coincide with the days Jonty Dobson chose not to come to school. Had Jonty been there, Arthur would have remained inside, sitting at his desk for the entire day.

As he walked into the schoolhouse after lunch, Arthur knew something was wrong. Standing at the front of the class were Minister McCarty and Doctor Falvey. Both men wore somber looks, and the minister was shifting nervously, crumpling his hat in his hands. Mrs. Dumphry sat at her desk watching the men.

"Take your seats, children. Hurry up now," Mrs. Dumphry said in her high voice. "These two boys have something they would like to share with the class."

Doctor Falvey glanced at Mrs. Dumphry irritably. "We aren't boys anymore. I graduated twenty-eight years ago, and—"

Slam. Mrs. Dumphry's hand crashed down on her desk. Doctor Falvey jumped, and Minister McCarty let out a small squeal of fear.

"You know better than that, Patrick Falvey. You may address me as Mrs. Dumphry. Or would you like to stay after class for detention?"

Every student watched wide-eyed as the doctor opened his mouth angrily, then, seeing the look in Mrs. Dumphry's eyes, turned beet red and nodded. "Yes, ma'am," he said, shifting uncomfortably.

After a moment Mrs. Dumphry nodded. "As I was saying," she continued, "these boys have something they wish to share with you."

With a cautious look at Mrs. Dumphry, Minister McCarty stepped forward. "Just a few hours ago, something was found down by the river."

Arthur could tell the minister wasn't comfortable with the subject.

"At least three farmers have had livestock go missing over the past few days. At first they thought the animals had just wandered off. But early this morning, while Andy McGibbons was walking through the forest ..." The minister paused, paling slightly. "Well," he said, as he looked at the ground, "poor young Andrew found the missing animals." Minister McCarty stopped again, wiping sweat from his forehead as Doctor Falvey put a comforting hand on his shoulder.

Mrs. Dumphry snorted. "In all the years I taught you, did you boys learn nothing?" she chided. "Bad news only becomes worse when you delay it. Speak the truth, and be done with it."

Minister McCarty shot another irritable glance at Mrs. Dumphry before continuing. "Andy found a large pile of bones." The entire class gasped loudly, and then every child began talking at the same time. Some shouted questions, while others simply cried out in fear.

Minister McCarty and Doctor Falvey seemed overwhelmed by the outburst.

"Silence!" Mrs. Dumphry's voice was like the crack of a whip.

The voices cut off immediately, and each child watched their ancient teacher with wide eyes.

"Children, listen to me. Just last year I went swimming with the great white sharks. I tell you this to let you know that animals can smell fear. And whatever is killing these poor beasts will only be encouraged by the smell. You mustn't allow fear to rule you." Mrs. Dumphry beamed with pride. "I swam alongside those sharks for hours, and at no time did they sense even a smidgen of fear."

Arthur would have been willing to bet it had been the sharks that had been afraid.

"Patrick Falvey and George McCarty will escort every one of you to your homes. Over the next few days, or until we find the beast, school will be canceled. And remember, whatever happens, do not enter the forest."

Mrs. Dumphry grabbed an eraser and began clearing the chalkboard. Everyone just sat and watched with wide eyes, too afraid to move. After a moment Doctor Falvey shook his head and spoke to the class.

He cleared his throat. "Yes, well, ah … that's right," he said. "Come along now, children, and stay together."

Arthur didn't move. He sat at his desk staring fearfully out the window. Jack was out there. They'd promised to meet each other at their fort at the end of the school day. Feeling a sense of dread, Arthur decided it would be best to tell Mrs. Dumphry. Maybe she would go out and find his best friend.

Chapter 5

WITHIN THE CLOUD

At the best of times, Jack Staples was not the greatest athlete. But running full speed through the forest while being pursued by black fog had left him exhausted. He could barely breathe. He'd run harder and faster than ever before. As Jack lay beneath the ocean of darkness, he turned onto his back and struggled to fill his lungs.

The moment the dark fog crashed over him like a tidal wave, the whispering had stopped. And though the fog didn't make a sound, he could feel it above him. With the fog came a wind that gave Jack the feeling of being doused in sewage.

When a hand gripped Jack's shoulder, he screamed in fear. As he turned to see who it was, he would have screamed again if he hadn't been so confused. Lying beside Jack was … Jack. He was looking at himself. The other Jack was gripping his shoulder and weeping uncontrollably. His clothes were unlike anything Jack had seen before. He wore a black cloak and a shirt the color of a storm cloud with elaborate golden thread sewn into each shoulder. But what most drew Jack's eye was the sword in the other Jack's hand. Its blade was the color of pitch, and on its pommel was the head of a roaring lion.

The sword-bearing Jack screamed through tears, "You have to listen to them, do you hear me? You have to listen! It's you who kills them! You kill them all. Don't you understand? Mother, the town, the city of Agartha! Its all your fault, all of it!"

The weeping Jack pounced on Jack and began choking him. Jack fought with himself in a frenzied attempt to keep the other Jack's hands away from his neck.

"I can't let you live," the other Jack said, weeping. "Don't you understand? We destroy everything! The prophecy is about me. I am the one who will join the Assassin. I am the one who destroys the Awakened!"

The only thing Jack understood was that he was slowly losing the battle with himself. Above them, the dark fog continued to rage as its scorching wind blew a torrent of earth and leaves into the air. Just as Jack thought he was going to lose the battle, the other Jack screamed.

"No!"

This was the last word Jack heard before losing consciousness.

The words of Minister McCarty and Doctor Falvey spun through Arthur's mind as he entered the forest. He was more afraid than he had ever been, yet he knew he could not turn back. Jack was his best friend and would never have left him in the forest. Arthur had hoped to ask Mrs. Dumphry for help, but she'd left the schoolhouse as soon as the chalkboard had been erased.

He had then tried to tell Doctor Falvey about it, but the doctor refused to listen. "I am sure young Jack is safe at home, dear boy. No need to worry," he'd said as he patted Arthur on the head like a dog. So, with no other options that Arthur could see, he'd sneaked away to warn his friend of the monster lurking in the woods.

Arthur could hear the sounds of birds chirping and the wind blowing, and these sounds were okay; they were normal. But every now and then, he thought he heard a twig break or a whisper from somewhere in the trees. Each time this happened, he dropped to the ground or hid behind a bush, too afraid to move.

"No!" a voice screamed.

Arthur froze. The scream had come from somewhere deep in the woods. It hadn't sounded like Jack, but could he be sure?

"No! Why won't you listen to me?" the voice screamed again.

Arthur couldn't move. He wanted to run, to hide; but he knew he should try to help whoever was screaming. Besides that, he still needed to make sure Jack wasn't waiting at the fort. Just as he was about to step forward, a muddy hand shot out of the earth directly next to his foot. Screaming at the top of his lungs, Arthur turned to run and promptly tripped over his own feet.

He looked back in horror as the hand quickly resolved into an arm. Before he could move, the hand shot out and gripped Arthur's ankle, causing him to scream even louder as he tried to scramble away. Horrified, he watched the earth around the arm shift and swell. He nearly fainted when a terrible, beastly shape rose from the ground. Dirt and leaves fell everywhere, and the monster grew ever taller.

"Don't eat me!" Arthur shrieked.

The beast let go of his leg and shook a head that seemed to be made entirely of mud and tree limbs. Dirt and branches fell everywhere. Arthur squeezed his eyes shut. He had no doubt he would soon feel razor-sharp fangs sinking into him.

"What are you doing?" a voice called out.

Arthur didn't hear the voice; he was too busy begging. "Please, don't eat me. Please, I'm sure I don't taste very good."

"Arthur! It's me. What are you doing here? Why would I eat you?"

Arthur opened his eyes to see Jack kneeling beside him. He was covered in mud, with leaves and twigs sticking out of his hair and clothing.

"That wasn't funny!" Arthur shouted. "You scared me half to death!"

"I wasn't trying to scare you," Jack replied. "I just woke up this instant. It was the dark fog that put me here." He rubbed at his neck as if it were sore. "Did you see it? The black fog ... or ... or the other ... boy?"

Arthur was confused. "What do you mean you woke up here? What black fog?"

Before Jack could answer, a beastly roar resounded through the forest.

"The beast!" Arthur cried.

"The fog!" Jack said as a second roar sounded, and this time it was closer. Without another word, the boys shared a fearful look, turned, and ran toward the schoolhouse. Not far behind, Arthur could hear the loud crashing of branches.

Arthur half ran, half stumbled through the forest, yet he wasn't as fast as his friend, and he began to fall behind.

"We're almost there!" Jack yelled encouragingly.

The beast was closer now, so close that Arthur was sure it would be on him at any moment. As he ran, something high up in the trees caught his eye. When he glanced upward, he saw a flash of deep red passing between trees. Whatever it was, it easily kept pace with them.

As his eyes were focused upward, Arthur's foot caught on a root, causing him to fall flat on his face. He gasped for breath, frantically rolling onto his back. Before he could think to stand, the beast arrived and skidded to a stop less than twenty paces away. Although it was hidden in the shadows of the sinking sun, Arthur could tell it was enormous. It had a mammoth head and fierce yellow eyes.

From somewhere high up in the trees, a small shape dropped from branch to branch, spinning around one only to jump to the next. What looked like crimson wings floated and swirled as it dropped toward the ground.

As it landed directly between Arthur and the beast, Arthur realized it was not a bird but a girl in a crimson cloak. The girl shot

Arthur an angry look before turning to face the beast. She had raven-black hair and emerald eyes, and looked to be two or three years older than he and Jack.

Without ever taking her eyes off the beast, the girl called out, "You both need to get out of here! I can't keep him away forever!"

Arthur looked up to see Jack by his side. His best friend's eyes were glued to the girl. "I know her," Jack said.

Arthur didn't care who she was; all he cared about was getting safely away from the beast. He grabbed Jack's hand and stood. Very slowly, both boys began walking backward. Arthur feared what might happen if they turned their backs on the beast.

"Go!" the girl yelled.

Before Arthur could make himself run, the beast let out a thunderous roar and leaped from the shadows. The red-cloaked girl dropped and rolled out of its way, screaming, "Run!"

Arthur gasped. The beast was a black-maned lion! As he turned to run, Arthur saw Jack sit down. "What are you doing?" Arthur screamed. "We need to go!" But Jack didn't move. He didn't even blink. He just sat there, shifting his gaze between the girl and the lion.

"It's you!" Jack gasped at the girl.

Chapter 6

A BIRTHDAY TO
REMEMBER

Eight years earlier

Alexia Dreager had been a tomboy from the day she was born. When she was only six months old, she would scrunch up her face and cry whenever her parents dressed her in anything even slightly pretty.

As she grew older, her parents tried to teach her to act like a "proper lady," but every chance she got, she would be off climbing something or playing in the mud. Alexia preferred play-fighting to dolls, and only once in her life did she willingly wear a dress.

On the morning of her birthday, Alexia woke up well before the sun and was thrilled to finally be turning five! Sprinting into her parents' bedroom, she leaped onto their bed and landed on her father's chest.

"It's my birthday!" she shouted. Alexia had spent the whole night dreaming of sword fights, slings, and a new climbing rope. She couldn't wait to open her presents.

"Slow down there, Ally Goat," her father said, laughing. "Look how big you grew last night; you must have turned five while I wasn't looking."

Alexia smiled excitedly. She loved it when he called her Ally Goat. He'd come up with the nickname when he saw her climbing a large and very high boulder. After watching for a moment, he ran over, scooped her up, and told her that her new name was Ally Goat because she climbed better than any goat he'd ever seen.

"I'm guessing you'll be wanting your presents, then?" her father asked with a grin.

"I can't wait!" Alexia jumped up and down on the bed.

Her mother smiled ruefully. "This year, my sweet Alexia, we have something very special to give you."

"I know you wanted a sling," her father said, "but what you are about to open will make you look like a princess."

Alexia wrinkled her nose. Sometimes her parents made her play with the girl who lived down the road, Sarah Cryst, who was the same age. Sarah loved to play dress-up. Alexia didn't understand the game. All you did was try on different clothes over and over again. Sarah would try on outfit after outfit and then dance around and talk about being a "princess," or she'd want to play "wedding."

Her mother saw her scrunched-up face and burst into laughter. "You are our greatest gift, my girl. You are my moon and my stars, and I made this present for you myself."

Alexia took the present. It was small and had a pink bow on top. Although she didn't care about looking like a princess, she was excited to be given something her mother had made.

"Okay, my little goat," her father said and chuckled. "Open it."

As she ripped through the brown paper, the expression on her face shifted from excitement to confusion. In the box was a dress. It was deep crimson with black trim. She looked at the dress for a moment before setting it on her lap. She knew she should say thank you. She knew she should hug her mother and father and not be rude, but she couldn't help herself. Alexia began to cry.

Both of her parents burst into laughter. Soon they were laughing so hard they were also crying! "Oh, my Ally Goat," her father said, hugging her close. "Don't ever change." After reaching behind his back, he handed her one more present. At the sight of the second gift, she smiled excitedly and wiped the tears from her eyes. She'd never had more than one present before!

Alexia tore at the paper wrapping. Inside was a brand-new sling. "I don't have the skills to make a dress, but I did make the sling," her father said. Alexia immediately began swinging it around. She could tell her father was a master craftsman.

"Not in the house, young lady." Her mother snatched it out of the air.

Alexia laughed as she gave both of her parents a big hug.

Yet it wasn't the dress or the sling that made Alexia's fifth birthday so memorable. A short while after she'd opened her presents, Alexia ran upstairs to change. Although she didn't love the idea of wearing dresses, this dress was different. Her mother had made it for her.

As she pulled the dress over her head, her bright green eyes fell on the sling lying on her bed. She quickly closed her bedroom door, grabbed the sling, and climbed out her window and down the maple tree. *I'll go for just a few minutes,* she thought. *They won't even know I'm gone.*

Wearing her new red dress and with her sling tucked into her belt, Alexia ran into the woods. She spent an hour searching for the perfect stones to shoot at the birds and squirrels. She then spent another hour hunting down and shooting at the birds and squirrels. It was after she'd hit her seventeenth squirrel that Alexia realized she'd been gone far too long. Suddenly worried she would get into trouble, she began to run.

Alexia sprinted onto the road leading to her house. Rising high into the cloudless sky was a large plume of smoke. Tears sprang to her eyes as she topped the small hill and saw that her house was on fire.

Alexia began to scream, "Mother! Father! I'm here! Where are you?" As she approached the house, the flames were scorching. Even from the middle of the path, she could feel her skin beginning to burn, yet she didn't care. She continued forward as hot tears streamed down her cheeks. "Mother! Father! I'm here!"

Alexia's clothing began to smoke, yet still she walked closer. And when the heat finally became too much for her, she collapsed.

When she opened her eyes, Alexia was weary beyond words, and her body felt as though it had been beaten for hours. Her skin burned, and her eyes stung. At first she didn't understand what she was seeing.

"That looks like my house," she croaked, her throat feeling as dry as a desert. "Except ..." The house she was looking down on had been burned to the ground. Only the tall chimney rising from a stone fireplace was still standing.

As she remembered the fire, Alexia bolted upright. Only then did she realize she was sitting on the highest branch of a tall oak tree. Dizzy and confused, she burst into tears as she grabbed the branch, lying flat and holding on with all her might.

After some time passed, Alexia began to remember that she was not just Alexia Dreager, a five-year-old girl. She was Ally Goat, and she was the best climber her father had ever seen. She would climb down this tree. And when she arrived at the bottom, her mother and father would be waiting for her.

A short while later, Alexia neared the lower branches of the tree. She stopped for a moment and took a deep breath. Until now, she hadn't allowed herself to think of anything other than getting down. Now that she was close, she began to fear her parents might not be waiting for her. *Surely they should be looking for me by now.*

When she heard the sound of Irish pipes, she called out excitedly, "Father! I'm here!" Her father was well known as the best piper in all of Ireland. "Father, I'm all right! I'm in the tree!" she said. Yet the pipes continued.

Without thinking, Alexia dove from her branch. She didn't have much time to think about what she'd just done, so she quickly tucked her head into her chest and thrust her arms out in front of her. As she hit the ground, she rolled into a somersault, and then another, then another.

Shocked, Alexia rolled to her feet and looked up at the branch she'd been standing on. "What was I thinking?" she asked aloud. But it didn't matter. Nothing mattered now except her mother and father. *They must be worried sick about me.* She grinned at the thought of their pleasure at seeing her and ran toward the sound of the bagpipes.

As she neared the edge of the woods, Alexia froze. What she saw took her breath away. A large group of men and women had gathered. Everyone wore black and were standing around three freshly dug graves. In the middle of the crowd, two men sat on chairs, playing their bagpipes. Both were far shorter and fatter than her father. Alexia had been to a funeral before, and she knew what this meant. It was custom to bury those who died near to where they had lived.

Scrubbing at the tears on her soot-stained cheeks, Alexia was unable to make herself move. She sat watching the three graves long after all the mourners left. As the sun was setting, she finally worked up the courage to walk over to them.

A small wooden placard had been placed on a post at the head of each grave. Although she couldn't read, Alexia knew what they were for. The one at the head of the largest mound would have her father's name, and the other, at the head of the slightly smaller mound, would have her mother's. As she looked at them, Alexia could barely breathe.

With nothing but horror in the pit of her stomach, she stumbled forward, feeling as if she were in a dream. She now stood before the third and smallest mound. Although she couldn't read all the words, she could read her name: "Alexia, 'Ally Goat' Dreager." She dropped to her knees, the shock too much to bear. Her parents were dead, and apparently, everyone thought she had died as well.

She stayed by the graves long past sunset. She knew she should find someone and tell them she was alive, but she had no family left. Her only uncle had died before she was born and her grandparents when she was just a baby. As the hours passed, a stony look entered her eyes. When she finally stood and walked back into the forest, she had one thought echoing through her mind: *I don't need anyone to look after me. I don't need anyone at all.*

Alexia spent the next few years on her own, stealing food and clothes and sleeping high up in the trees. Even on the nights she didn't fall asleep in a tree, she often woke up in one. Before long the trees had become her home, and she felt far more comfortable in their branches than on the ground.

A few months after she turned twelve, Alexia found herself in the grand city of Belfast. She spent her nights sleeping on rooftops and her days stealing food. When the circus came to town, Alexia happened to be in the right place at the right time and was offered a job. The circus master had initially hired her to clean up after the elephants, but on the day he walked in and caught her doing backflips on the tumblers' rope, everything changed.

Alexia quickly found herself starring in the biggest show in the history of the circus. The show involved four torch-bearing tumblers, a ring of fire, two lions, and Alexia. She was absolutely thrilled with the turn of events, especially about the lions. Over time, the beasts became two of her very best friends. And for the first time in many years, she once again had a family of her own.

On the night of the circus fire, everything changed for Alexia again. After the fire, the circus was shut down. Every tumbler had broken an arm or a leg, and most of the animals had escaped. Even worse, one of Alexia's best friends, the lion she'd named Beast, had died in the fire. The moment she'd learned the second lion—the one she'd named Killer—had escaped, Alexia set out in search of her furry friend.

Two days after the fire, she found Killer. Alexia was surprised and somewhat hurt to discover that the lion wouldn't follow her back to the circus. He was happy to play hide-and-seek and still loved being scratched behind the ears, yet no matter how hard she tried, she could not make the beast leave the forest that surrounded the sleepy town of Ballylesson.

Alexia spent most of her time trying to keep Killer away from the townsfolk. If they found out a lion was loose in the woods, they would surely come out and try to kill it. Every time Killer ate a farm animal, Alexia would drag the bones off to a hiding place she'd found down by the river. This was a disgusting job she disliked very much.

After five days in the forest outside Ballylesson, Alexia decided enough was enough. Whether he wanted to or not, she would take Killer back to the circus and demand that the circus master reopen the show. Just as Alexia was about to try to corral the lion, she heard someone scream. Killer immediately bolted away to see what was happening.

Furious that her lion friend wouldn't listen, and afraid of what would happen if one of the townsfolk saw him, Alexia chased him through the woods. Before long, she came upon two boys who were running for their lives, desperate to escape the pursuing lion.

Chapter 7

THE CHOICE
OF A BEAST

"What are you doing?" the girl in red yelled at Jack. "You need to run!"

But Jack was far too stunned to move. "It's the second lion," he whispered.

As the beast roared again, its eyes stayed locked on Jack. Five days earlier, the golden-maned lion had died saving him, and though Jack had thought about it many times since, he still didn't understand why.

"Whatever you do," the girl spoke in a hushed tone, "don't—"

With a fierce snarl, the lion pounced, landing on top of Jack with its massive paws pinning him to the ground.

"Don't look him in the eye." The girl's voice was tight with fear. "If you do, he'll see it as a challenge."

The lion's growling grew even more threatening as it brought its head close to Jack's chest and inhaled deeply. When the beast roared again, Jack squeezed his eyes shut, trembling at the hot breath on his face.

"You need to help him," Arthur screamed at the girl. "You have to do something!"

"What do you think I'm doing?" she shot back. "If you had run away like I told you, this wouldn't be happening."

The lion continued its study of Jack, ignoring Arthur and the girl. Jack wanted to scream as the beast snapped its jaws just in front of his nose. He tried to stay calm as another, lower growl erupted from deep inside the lion's chest.

"Boy, just don't move. I am going to try and …" The girl was suddenly speechless as the lion shook its head, uncurled its tongue, and began licking Jack on the face.

"What?" the girl said, gasping.

The beast's tongue slid roughly across Jack's cheek and forehead, then down his neck. As it licked him, the lion began to purr loudly. The tongue continued to slide over his face, and Jack didn't move. He was frozen in fear with no idea what was happening. A moment later, the beast snarled at the girl, then gave Jack a knowing look before bounding away to disappear into the forest.

Jack lay flat on his back, trying to comprehend what just happened. For a long moment he didn't move, and neither Arthur nor the girl said a word. As he sat up, he touched his face in disbelief.

"Well, that was weird," Arthur said, turning to the girl. "What on earth are you doing with a lion? You know they're dangerous, right?"

"She was the one who walked the tightrope on the night of the fire," Jack said. "I told you about her."

"You were there?" the girl broke in. "You were at the circus?" She turned to Jack with a dangerous look in her eyes.

"I was there," he said slowly. "I'm the boy the other lion saved from the fire."

The girl threw out her arm, pointing her finger in accusation. "It was you!"

Jack stepped back from the girl's sudden rage, blinking in confusion.

"You killed him!" she screamed as she grabbed a sling from her belt and spun it around threateningly. "That lion was my best friend, boy! I knew I'd find you someday. Prepare to die." The girl glared at Jack, spinning the sling faster.

"He was your friend?" Jack felt sick to his stomach.

The girl didn't answer but kept her sling spinning.

"I think he … I think he could have escaped. I've thought about it many times. I think he could have gotten away from the fire, but he didn't. He chose to save me instead."

The girl's face contorted in rage.

"I'm sorry you lost your friend. I'm sorry he—"

Thwang. The stone hurtled from her sling, flying directly at Jack's head.

As the girl's stone flew toward him, something quite strange happened. From behind a nearby bush catapulted a much larger stone, also flying toward Jack's head. When the girl's stone was about to strike Jack flat on the nose, the larger stone collided with it, deflecting it away at the last possible moment.

Jack blinked and shared a look of shock with both Arthur and the girl. All three children turned to look toward the bush. None of them moved or said a word, even when the slight whooshing sound came from above. Jack looked up to see a small stone dropping toward the girl. The girl was squinting directly into the setting sun, so she never saw the stone that struck her on the top of her head, knocking her unconscious.

Jack and his best friend stared at the girl, then at each other. "What had just happened?" Jack breathed.

"My, my, isn't she a wild one?" Walking spryly from behind the bush was Mrs. Dumphry. In her hands was a sling only slightly longer than the one still clutched in the girl's hand.

"Mrs. Dumphry?" Arthur croaked. "What are you doing here?"

Mrs. Dumphry snorted loudly as she walked over to the girl. "Do you think to question me, child? Does the badger waste its breath on the bear?"

Arthur opened his mouth to speak, then promptly closed it again, unsure how to respond. Mrs. Dumphry knelt and placed a hand on the girl's forehead, wiping off a bit of grime.

"I don't know what's worse—young Mr. Greaves ignoring my instructions or ..." As she was speaking, Mrs. Dumphry placed her thumb under the girl's eye and pulled it open. The second she had it opened, she whipped her hand away and hissed sharply.

"Mrs. Dumphry, what's wrong?" Jack hadn't thought anything could shock his ancient teacher. But she didn't answer; she stayed kneeling with an unbelieving look painting her face. "Mrs. Dumphry?" Jack asked again.

"Silence!" Her voice held a note of alarm. "Who is this girl? Speak now, and speak truthfully."

"I don't know her name, but she used to work at the circus. She was the one who walked the tightrope."

After a moment, Mrs. Dumphry's hand hesitantly made its way back to the girl's eye. With her index finger she once again pulled at the skin, bringing her face closer to get a better look. "It's not possible," she whispered. "Two children born without scales?" For a long moment, she sat unmoving. Her eyes were squeezed shut, and Jack was beginning to wonder if she'd fallen asleep. By the look on Arthur's face, it was clear he was thinking the same.

Just as Jack opened his mouth to speak again, Mrs. Dumphry's shoulders began to shake. It seemed to Jack that she was both laughing and crying at the same time. Arthur glanced at Jack and raised an eyebrow.

"It's time to go," Mrs. Dumphry said. She stood and began walking toward the schoolhouse.

After a moment Jack called after her, "We can't just leave her here!"

Mrs. Dumphry turned and looked back. "Wise men speak because they have something to say; fools speak because they have to say something. Which are you, child?"

Jack shuffled his feet. "It's just ... I don't think we should leave her."

"Well, of course not. But a true leader does not need to be asked to do the right thing; he does it." She turned and continued walking toward the school.

Jack watched her go, utterly confused.

"I guess that means we have to carry her," Arthur offered.

Both boys lifted the girl between them, one of her arms over each of their shoulders. With her feet dragging along the forest floor behind them, they stumbled forward, doing their best not to lose sight of Mrs. Dumphry. But within the first minute, their ancient teacher was nowhere to be seen.

Chapter 8

THE BIRTH OF
THE ASSASSIN

Darkness had fallen by the time Jack and Arthur stumbled into the schoolhouse, dragging the red-cloaked girl between them. She was covered in mud from when the boys had dropped her, face-first, into a puddle. It hadn't been on purpose. A rabbit had been scared from its hole and leaped out in front of them. Both boys had screamed in fear and dropped the poor girl without thinking.

Once inside, Jack was glad to see a fire already burning in the hearth, though Mrs. Dumphry was nowhere to be seen.

"You don't think she went home for the night, do you?" Arthur's voice trembled slightly.

"I don't think she'd leave us here." Jack was skeptical. "Maybe she just went to fetch some wood or something."

With fear weighing heavy on his mind, the firelight made the once-familiar schoolhouse more unnerving than warm. Shadows jumped and danced as the light shifted continuously. More than once, Jack was certain he saw dark fog slithering across the floor, yet each time he looked, there was nothing there.

As the boys carried the girl to the fire, they tracked thick, muddy footprints across the entire length of the room. And as he passed Mrs. Dumphry's desk, Jack noticed a large number of odd-looking papers scattered across it.

"Why do you think she hates you so much?" Arthur motioned to the muddy girl as they laid her next to the fire.

"I told you already—she thinks I killed the lion."

"You'd think she'd be happy you killed the lion!"

"I didn't kill it," Jack said angrily. "I ... I don't know what happened."

"I'm just saying she's mad, that's all." Arthur glanced at her as he sat on a nearby chair. "Anyone who considers a lion to be their 'best friend' is as loony as a loon."

Jack had to agree; she did look rather mad with her face all muddy and the firelight casting deep shadows on one side.

"Either way, she's Mrs. Dumphry's problem now, assuming she ever comes back," Arthur said.

Too agitated to sit, Jack made his way to Mrs. Dumphry's desk. There was something odd about it. His teacher was the most orderly woman he'd ever met. Her voice rang in his head, *"An unordered desk points to an undisciplined mind."*

"The thing is"—Arthur sat facing the fire with his back to Jack—"this girl isn't right. Just look at how she's dressed. It's not proper!"

The flickering firelight only partially illuminated the desk, so at first, Jack had trouble understanding what he was seeing.

"A girl should wear a dress, not trousers." Arthur's voice became higher by the second as he rambled on.

Quickly pushing Arthur out of his mind, Jack stared at a large number of cracked brown pages scattered across Mrs. Dumphry's desk. The papers looked haphazard, overlapping one another and covering most of the surface, leaving only the edges bare. It seemed to Jack as if this had been done purposefully, though he couldn't imagine why. Even though every page was a separate piece, they were linked in a way he didn't understand. Covering the pages was a strange picture.

"It can't be," he said, though he was speaking to himself.

"That's what I'm saying," Arthur said. "You'd think she'd at least speak like a proper girl. And can you believe she carries a sling? A sling for goodness sake! And, I ask you, what kind of girl goes about climbing trees like that?"

Jack didn't hear a word Arthur was saying; he was much too engrossed in the pages. The longer he looked, the more sure he was that it wasn't a picture; it was a map of some sort. Great mountain ranges had been drawn, crossing several pages. Yet where the pages overlapped one another, the mountains seemed to rise upward, almost as if they came off the actual pages.

It reminded Jack of the pop-out book he'd seen at Mr. Hamilton's bookstore last summer. When he'd opened the book, the characters inside had quite literally popped out, though they had been made of paper. Yet that book was nothing like what he was seeing now. The mountains linking the pages looked real. He was sure he could see snow falling on their peaks! As the mountains carried on into the middle of the pages, they once again became normal drawings.

Surrounding the mountains were large bodies of water. And where the pages overlapped, waves crashed, sending sprays into the air. Jack's jaw dropped. The water was the color of … he didn't know. He'd never seen anything like it. It wasn't just one color—there were hundreds of them, and Jack couldn't have named a single one. He began to laugh. The colors were dancing with one another as they spun in intricate patterns.

When Arthur heard him laugh, he glanced back in irritation. "Well, I don't think it's funny at all," he said. "She could have killed you with that stone!"

Jack ignored his friend. He scanned the map and began to grin. It was so beautiful! The longer he looked, the giddier he felt. He placed his hands on the desk, leaning in to get a closer look. As he leaned in, Jack had a vision. Whether it was in his head or he was watching it play out in the center of the map, he couldn't tell, but a scene began to flash before him.

There was a being made entirely of light. It was brighter than the sun and standing on the topmost peak of an enormous mountain. Whoever or whatever this being was, it was far too bright for Jack's eyes. Even when he squeezed them shut, he could still see the blinding light. As he tried to turn away, the being's voice boomed inside his head.

"I WILL ASCEND THE UTMOST HEIGHTS OF SIYYON." It was the most beautiful voice Jack had ever heard—every word sounded like a magnificent symphony.

"I AM BELIAL, THE LORD OF HARMONY. EVEN THE GREATEST DRAKEONS TREMBLE IN MY SIGHT. THE STARS BOW DOWN AND WORSHIP ME!"

The voice was so bewitching, so melodic, it took his breath away. Although the voice was echoing inside his head, Jack was sure the being wasn't talking to him.

"IF I RISE UP, THEY WILL FOLLOW. IF I MOVE NOW, I WILL UNSEAT THE AUTHOR HIMSELF!"

Although he didn't understand what they meant, Jack knew the words were wrong. Whoever Belial was, he had to feel it too. It was like the time Jack lied to his mother about eating the apple pie. When he told her he hadn't done it, he'd felt the words as they left his mouth. He'd known they were wrong before they formed on his tongue. Whoever was speaking, his words were like that. Except these words made Jack feel infinitely worse. Surely this strange being must feel it too.

"NOTHING IN ALL CREATION CAN BEAR TO LOOK UPON MY GLORY."

Then, Belial began to sing. If his speaking had been both beautiful and terrifying, his singing was infinitely more so. It made Jack want to dance and weep at the same time. The song had such beauty, such foreboding, that it felt as if all of creation were holding its breath.

As Belial sang, Jack collapsed onto the desk. When he opened his eyes, he was no longer in the schoolhouse in Ballylesson, Ireland, but was now on the top of a great mountain, standing behind Belial himself. Belial was still singing the same song.

Jack looked around in wonder. There was no sun in the sky, yet light radiated from the mountain. Every tree, rock, and blade of grass vibrated with the most beautiful light. The mountain was so high that Jack could see forever, and he stood on the edge of a sheer drop.

Although Belial was still bright, something had changed. His light was turning dark. It wasn't fading, but shifting to a different sort of light altogether. And in the sky above, tens of thousands of stars rained down.

As Jack watched the stars, images flashed in the sky. There were so many that he struggled to take them in. One was an image of himself. He was cradled in the arms of a creature with milky white eyes and black wings.

Next, he saw the girl in the crimson cloak running for her life. He couldn't see who was chasing her, but there was no doubt in his mind that she would be captured by something terribly evil.

In another vision, Arthur Greaves stood at the entrance to a city of nightmares. Then, Jack saw his father hiding a small wooden box beneath a pile of stones; next, his brother, Parker, appeared, standing on the edge of a cliff as a number of trees glided toward him.

More images flashed, but Jack could barely make them out. A wild-eyed boy holding a bow; a beast that was part wolf and part snake; a city made entirely of chambers and bridges; a small log cabin on the sea; a young girl with emerald eyes; a feathered pen that had been snapped in two; a mountain crumbling into the sea; a young girl with whimsical eyes; a dark cloud that swallowed the sky; and still more images flashed, faster and faster.

"YOU ARE LIKE … HIM!" The voice exploded like thunder.

Jack turned from the vision to see Belial standing a few paces away and looking directly at him. In Belial's eyes was a look of both hunger and fear. Yet he had changed with the singing of the song. His light had fused with darkness, and though he was still bright, Jack could look directly at him. It wasn't just Belial that had changed, though; the entire world was different. It felt somehow more … dangerous.

"YOU ARE LIKE THE AUTHOR HIMSELF." Belial was studying Jack, and though his voice was filled with rage, there was wariness in his eyes. Lifting his head, he screamed at the heavens, "THIS IS YOUR PLAN? THIS IS HOW YOU FIGHT BACK? A CHILD?"

Jack wanted to run, to hide, but he was already backed up against the edge of the cliff. One more step and he would fall to his death.

Belial looked at Jack and grinned. "I HAVE GREAT PLANS FOR YOU. I AM BELIAL, THE LORD OF HARMONY, AND I MARK YOU AS MINE."

Belial reached out and placed his finger on Jack's chest. And where his finger touched, a small trail of smoke began to rise. Screaming in pain and blinded by fear, Jack leaped from the cliff. As he plummeted downward, Belial called out.

"I AM COMING, BOY! YOU CANNOT HIDE FOREVER."

Jack hit the ground hard, biting his lip as his chin bounced on the floorboards. He was lying beside Mrs. Dumphry's desk. The fire crackled and popped. Arthur spoke loudly.

"Which is why you'd think she would just put on a bonnet or some kind of dress to—" Arthur stopped midsentence and leaped to his feet when he saw Jack lying face-first on the schoolhouse floor.

Chapter 9

A BAD DREAM

Jack was lying on the floor and could taste blood from where he'd bitten his lower lip when he landed. Unsure of whether he'd awakened from a nightmare or if he was going insane, he sat up.

Arthur was standing beside him. "What are you doing down there?"

Jack felt his chest. A small, half-moon–shaped hole had been burned into his shirt from where the strange being had touched him. Yet when he pulled the shirt aside, there wasn't a mark on him.

"How'd that happen?"

"I ... I don't know," Jack lied. He was careful not to disturb the contents on the desk as he stood. He trusted Arthur completely, but the events of the day were making his head spin. The dark fog, the other Jack who'd tried to kill him, and now the map all were making him feel very uncomfortable.

The papers still lay scattered across Mrs. Dumphry's desk, but every one of them was blank. Jack took a step back. "I think I might be sick," he said.

"If you are sick, then I am a spring chicken," Mrs. Dumphry said wryly.

Both boys jumped, turning to see their teacher sitting in her rocking chair by the fire.

"What you saw was a Masc Tinneas. It is a map of sorts, though it does not show where, but when. This map always reveals both the past and future." Mrs. Dumphry stood and poked the fire with her walking stick. "Tell me, child, what did the Masc Tinneas reveal to you?"

Jack had no reason to fear his teacher. She'd always been kind and was a close friend of his mother and father. She often came by the house to visit, though it was usually after Jack was already in bed. He'd spent many a night falling asleep at the top of the stairs listening to Mrs. Dumphry and his parents talk. But the idea of telling his teacher what he saw was unnerving.

Jack remembered what happened five years earlier. Mrs. Dumphry had sent a boy named Ethan Wild to the asylum. Ethan had been one of the older students at the Ballylesson Schoolhouse. One day during class he had gone mad, clutching at his eyes and rolling on the floor. Ethan kept screaming over and over again about the "searing light."

Every student had stood against the far wall, watching Ethan writhe and claw at his eyes. That was the last day he'd been seen in

Ballylesson. Everyone around town said Mrs. Dumphry had person-ally taken him to the asylum all the way out in Wallydrom, at least three days' ride from the town. With this memory clear in his mind, Jack decided it best he not tell his teacher anything at all.

Yet Mrs. Dumphry wasn't the type of woman you kept waiting. Everyone in Ballylesson sat up straighter when she walked into a room, and even Jack's mother spoke to her only with the utmost respect.

"My mother is probably worried sick by now," Jack said as he looked longingly at the front door. "I was supposed to be home ages ago."

"Your parents are on their way." Mrs. Dumphry's voice held a demanding tone. "They will be here momentarily. You need to tell me what you saw, child."

Jack felt like a worm being studied by a bird. "I d-didn't see any-thing," he stammered. "I-I don't know what you're talking about."

Out of the corner of his eye, Jack saw something dark slithering across the schoolhouse floor. "The dark fog!" he screamed as he ran back a few steps. But when he looked again, there was no fog, merely Whinny, the black cat that lived beneath the schoolhouse.

Mrs. Dumphry's eyes never left Jack. After a moment she let out a long, slow breath. "After so long, can this be how it begins? Can we have been so blind?" Her voice came out in a whisper. "Two children?" She sounded amazed. Mrs. Dumphry looked from the girl to Jack. "Child, you must tell me when and where you saw this dark fog. If the Shadowfog is here, then the entire town is in grave danger."

Jack felt his chest tighten. Part of him had hoped he was crazy. But Mrs. Dumphry's reaction was far too serious. "Just a few hours a-ago," he said. "It was in the woods just outside the school."

Arthur began muttering under his breath. "Dark fog, lions, crazy girls, and maps. What's going on?"

"With the Author's blessing, we are not too late," Mrs. Dumphry said. "What you saw has many names; some call it 'Shadowfog' or the 'Assassin's Cloud' or 'Black Death' to name a few. Regardless of its name, it is pure evil." Mrs. Dumphry stepped closer. "Tell me, how have you been feeling since the circus fire?"

The question took Jack by surprise, yet before he could say anything, Mrs. Dumphry continued, "There is much to be done before morning." Glancing at the mud on the floor, she spoke in a brusque tone, "Both of you have tracked mud into my school-house. When I return from my trip, you will each write, 'I will not treat the schoolhouse like a barnyard,' one hundred times on the blackboard."

Before either of the boys could think how to respond, Mrs. Dumphry turned toward the front entry. "Ah, it seems your parents have arrived." Without another word she walked out the back door.

The boys just stared at the door with their mouths opened wide. A moment later, Arthur's parents and Jack's mother entered through the front.

"Arthur Reginald Alexander Greaves, just what do you think you're doing?" Arthur's mother was a large woman, yet much of her size was muscle that just so happened to be covered by a thin layer of fat. His father was even larger, but in his case, it was all muscle. Arthur's father had spent his childhood as a blacksmith's apprentice, and the muscles he'd gained in that time had not gone away. Mr. Greaves now worked as a tanner, but he still forged his own horseshoes.

Arthur opened his mouth to speak, but his mother cut him off. "Minister McCarty told us about the beast in the woods! When you didn't come home, well, I thought ... I thought ..." When Arthur's mother burst into tears, so did he. Without another word he ran into her open arms.

"What were you thinking, Jack?" Jack's mother asked. "On your first time out since the fire, you pull a stunt like this!"

Jack didn't know what to say. Had it only been a few hours since he'd left the house? It felt like a lifetime ago. Hot tears sprang to his eyes.

"I was—" Jack stopped. "I didn't—" He cut off again, unsure what to say.

His mother walked over and wrapped him in a hug. "I was worried about you, especially after we heard about the beast in—" His mother stopped midsentence. Jack couldn't see her face, but he felt her body tense. As he stepped back, he saw that she was looking at the girl lying by the fire.

"Jacksie, who is that?"

Jack had forgotten all about the girl. "She's—"

"She is the one who was chasing the lion!" Arthur burst out excitedly. "And she can climb a tree like you wouldn't believe. And when she tried to kill Jack with a stone, Mrs. Dumphry saved him. You should have seen it!" Arthur stepped away from his mother, becoming more animated by the second. "She wasn't this dirty before, but Jack and I dropped her in the mud when we were trying to get back to the school. She is actually quite beautiful." Arthur stared at her, lost in thought, but before anyone could say a word, he began again.

"When I first saw her, I thought she was a boy. Can you believe that? She's far too pretty to be a boy. But then the lion came and jumped on Jack, and she"—Arthur motioned to the girl excitedly— "tried to save him. She is very brave. Except Jack didn't need her help because the lion apparently just wanted to lick him!" He threw his arms in the air.

Arthur was breathing heavily now, his eyes wide as he remembered the events of the day. Jack's mother walked to the girl and knelt beside her. "Oh yeah," Arthur continued, "when we got back, Mrs. Dumphry was acting crazy! She's going to make us write lines for tracking mud into the school, but it was only muddy because she left the girl in the woods in the first place." Arthur shook his head dramatically.

"There's a … lion in the woods?" Arthur's father sounded more incredulous than believing.

"It licked Jack?" Arthur's mother was clearly alarmed.

Before anyone could say a word, Jack broke in. "She's the girl from the circus, Mother—the one who was walking the tightrope."

Jack's mother had placed the girl's head on her lap and was running a hand through her hair. He couldn't see his mother's face, but he could tell something was wrong. Was she crying?

"Megan, what wrong?" Mrs. Greaves asked, stepping toward her.

Standing quickly, Jack's mother dabbed at her eyes and began to laugh. "Nothing! Absolutely nothing."

"You know this girl?" Mr. Greaves asked.

His mother didn't answer, but changed the subject. "I assume Mrs. Dumphry has gone, then?"

Jack nodded, confused.

"For the time being at least, this girl needs somewhere to stay. She will come home with us until we can find her parents." She looked at Mr. Greaves. "Would you mind carrying her out to the wagon? Jack and I will clear a space in the back."

"Of course," Mr. Greaves said. "Whatever you need. And, Megan, you will let us know if there's anything we can do. We are more than willing to help with the girl."

"Thank you, but I am sure we will be fine. It's late, and apparently"—she offered a rueful smile—"there's a lion on the loose. It's past time we all returned home."

Alexia ran through a field of blood-red flowers. The sun shone brightly overhead, and she felt … happy. It had been many years since she'd been truly happy—ever since the day of her fifth birthday.

She slowed at this thought. "What happened on my fifth birthday?" she wondered aloud. For a moment, she felt a stabbing in her heart, but just as quickly, the pain was gone. She darted forward again, laughing as she ran.

I'm going to pick some flowers for Mother. I just know she'll give me a big hug when I bring them home! Once again, the thought of her mother brought a sharp stabbing to Alexia's heart. Pushing it aside, she slowed and began collecting the most beautiful red wildflowers she'd ever seen. Laughing aloud, she grabbed armfuls of them, so many she was barely able to hold them all.

Mother will be so surprised. Why did the thought of her mother make her feel sad? For some reason, Alexia couldn't make her mind stand still.

Alexia suddenly realized she had no idea where she was. As she turned to look, her jaw dropped. In the valley below was an arena of sleek black stone that stood as tall as a mountain. As she looked at the arena, panic rose inside her. She felt it calling to her, willing her to come.

"I need to find Mother and Father," she whispered. "I need to tell them about the ..."

Fire.

Alexia dropped her armful of blood-red flowers. Why couldn't she remember? Something bad had happened. She placed her hands on her head.

Raging fire.

Dropping to her knees, Alexia was unable to breathe.

"NO!" she screamed. In the ground in front of her were three freshly dug graves.

"Mother!" Alexia shouted as she sat up in bed.

It took a moment to realize she'd been dreaming again. It was a dream she'd had many times since her fifth birthday, and each time she awoke, she experienced the heartache all over again. Yet this time, when she woke, she heard the voice of her mother.

"Ah, my girl. Everything is all right. You are here with us now, and it's going to be all right," her mother said as she ran her fingers through Alexia's hair.

Alexia was sitting in her bed in the darkness, and she couldn't believe it. Her mother was alive, and once again all was right with the world.

Chapter 10

TO SAVE A LIFE

"Mother!" Alexia screamed. Tears flowed down her cheeks as she jumped out of bed and hugged her mother tightly. "Mother! You're alive! And Father, is he here too?" She buried her face in her mother's chest, squeezing her tightly.

For a moment, her mother tensed, then slowly pushed herself back, holding Alexia by the shoulders.

"No ... I'm sorry, I ..." Something about her mother's voice sounded wrong to Alexia. "I didn't mean to make you think ..."

She felt as if a knife were slowly slicing into her belly. Alexia backed away, too afraid to speak.

Her mother struck a match, lighting a lamp on the bedside table. At first Alexia didn't understand what she was seeing.

"My girl, I am not your mother, but I am a friend. And I want to help you."

A deep rage welled inside Alexia. How dare this woman pretend to be her mother! How dare she trick her like that! Springing to her feet, she rounded on the woman, ready to punch, kick, or bite—it didn't matter. She was going to hit something.

The horrid woman stood but didn't back away. "I am sorry. I did not mean for you to think I was your … to think I …" A look of pain swept the woman's face as she stopped herself. "I am sorry that happened."

Alexia backed into the corner like a wounded animal.

"Is it true? Is your … did your mother and father—have they both passed away?" the woman asked.

Alexia snarled as her face contorted in rage. She was going to kill this woman. Reaching for the sling at her belt, she stopped. It wasn't there. The woman must have stolen it! That was the last gift her father had given her. And her clothes, her cloak. Where were they? This dreadful woman had stolen everything from her!

"All of your things are right here," the woman said, retrieving a small pile of clothes from the top of the dresser and holding them out to Alexia. "I cleaned them for you."

Alexia snatched her things from the woman's arms. "You can't keep me here," she said.

"I will not keep you from leaving," the woman replied. "You are free to go whenever you wish. But I want you to know that, if your family is gone, you will always have a home here, with us."

Alexia felt as if someone had punched her in the gut, but she ignored it. She opened her mouth to speak, but the woman cut her off. "I don't know how long you have been on your own, but you aren't alone anymore. Whatever you need, we will be here for you."

"I don't need anybody," Alexia muttered, angrily striding toward the door. "If you try to stop me, you'll regret it."

"Alexia!" the woman said boldly.

Alexia stopped. *How does she know my name?* Alexia hadn't told anyone her real name since her fifth birthday. She stood, frozen, unable to move.

"Alexia, I am not your—" The woman stopped and brushed away fresh tears. "I am not your mother. Nor do I think I would ever be able to take her place. I am sure she must have been a strong and beautiful woman and that she loved you more than the moon or the stars."

Alexia swallowed hard but didn't turn around. Her mother had often called her "my moon and stars." It had been one of her many nicknames.

"But I know she would want you to be taken care of. I have no doubt that you can take care of yourself, but it's not what she would have wanted."

Alexia didn't move. She wanted to run, she wanted to tell the woman to shut up, but she couldn't move. How dare she talk about her mother like that!

"Alexia," the woman said softly, "I can never hope to be anything like her, but I promise you this: I will love you as much as any mother has ever loved a child." The woman was crying now as she stepped forward. "You can leave if you like, but if you stay, you will be loved and cared for."

In an all-out rage, Alexia charged the woman. She pounded her with fists as she kicked and screamed. How dare she say these things!

The woman let Alexia punch and kick her. Yes, she blocked some of the more powerful strikes, but mostly she just stood and allowed herself to be beaten. Alexia was so desperately angry! She was angry with the woman, with her parents, with herself—maybe if she hadn't left the house, she could have stopped the fire. Maybe they had died because of her. Finally, her attack slowed, and in a moment of immense sorrow and exhaustion, she collapsed into the woman's arms and began to sob.

As she felt the woman's arms around her, Alexia screamed again. There was so much she wanted to say, and though she still wanted to hit the woman, more than anything, more than any other thought in her head, she wanted to be held by her. She wanted her to run her fingers through her hair and tell her everything was going to be all right.

And in the end, that is exactly what happened.

The next morning, Jack woke up filled with anticipation. He lay in bed remembering his dream, savoring every detail. "It was so real," he whispered. Shadowfog, a beautiful girl who climbed like a cat, a map that moved and transported him to another world ... It was all so wonderful.

He couldn't wait to tell Arthur and Parker. Arthur would absolutely love it, while Parker, Jack was sure, would simply roll his eyes and ask why he hadn't been in the dream. As Jack hopped out of bed to get dressed, he was surprised to find that more than half of his clothes were missing. *Maybe Mother is mending them*, he thought. Picking up the first things he found, he quickly dressed and sprinted through the hallway and down the stairs.

"Mother, you'll never guess what I dreamed last night!" Jack said, then grabbed the bannister and swung himself around. He ran full-tilt through the dining room and then saw his mother sitting at the kitchen table drinking her morning tea. Her lip was split and she had a black eye and a few cuts and scrapes on her arms, yet when she saw him coming, she smiled warmly.

"Mother, what happened to you?" As he entered the room, he saw someone sitting on the opposite side of the table. In an instant, he realized it was the girl from his dream. Trying to skid to a stop, he tripped and crashed into the table, sending food and hot tea flying.

"Jack," his mother said, grinning, "I trust you remember your friend from yesterday? Her name is Alexia and—"

Alexia jumped to her feet, shoving her chair back. "He is your son?" she shouted incredulously. "This is the boy I was telling you about! The one who killed my best friend!"

Jack crawled to his feet, still confused. "So yesterday wasn't a dream?" he asked, rubbing the bump beginning to rise on his forehead. "What do you mean, I killed your friend? You tried to kill me!"

Alexia balled her hands into fists and stepped forward threateningly. "I've beaten up boys twice my age," she snarled, "so this will be easy!"

Jack backed away fearfully. He'd seen Jonty Dobson start many fights, and he wasn't excited about being in one now. "She slung a rock at my head!" he yelled to his mother.

"Children! Stop this, right now. I will not have it in my house. Sit down!"

Jack sat right away. He had rarely heard his mother so angry. But Alexia stood her ground, staring daggers at Jack.

"You didn't tell me he was your son," she said fiercely.

"Alexia, when you told me about your friend who died in the circus fire, I wondered if you were talking about the lion who saved Jack's life, but I wasn't sure. I was going to ask you when you finished your story. Yet you know as well as I that it was not Jack who killed your friend, it was the fire. And though I wasn't sure I understood it until now, I think it must have been you who saved Jack—you and your lion friend." Tears shone in her eyes.

"What do you mean?" Alexia asked. "I've never seen him before yesterday."

"No, you never met Jack. But if the lion was your best friend, then I assume you spent many hours with him. I am sure you trained him for shows, you fed him, and you probably were the best friend a lion could have hoped for."

Alexia wiped a tear from her cheek as she turned to stare out the window. "He was my very best friend," she said. "I used to sneak into the cages at night and sleep between Beast and Killer. They looked after me. They took care of me." Alexia whispered the last words.

After a moment Jack's mother smiled sadly. "You see? It was because of you that ... Beast was it? Or Killer?" She smiled at the names.

"Beast," Alexia said sullenly.

"You were the reason Beast learned to love people. He loved you so much that he was willing to give his life to save someone like you. He chose to save my Jack because he was thinking of you."

Alexia opened her mouth, but nothing came out. Finally, she said, "I really miss them."

Jack's mother smiled and walked over, placing her hands on Alexia's shoulders. "Ah, Alexia, you are a godsend. It is because of you that Jack is alive."

Both Jack's mother and Alexia had tears in their eyes. And as he thought about it, Jack, too, began to cry. The lion had saved his life. It hadn't been a mistake; the beast had given its life to save him.

Chapter 11

EVERYTHING IS NORMAL

The following days were anything but normal. After his experience in the woods, let alone what happened in the schoolhouse, Jack was anxious about absolutely everything. He found himself jumping at every shifting shadow or unexpected noise.

Had any of it been real? Jack hadn't seen any more slithering fog or moving maps or other Jacks trying to kill him. *Is this what it feels like to go mad?* he wondered. At least three times a day his mother asked him if he was all right or if he wanted to talk. And he did want to talk, but he was afraid that she might think of him differently.

Ethan Wild, the boy who'd gone mad at the schoolhouse, had been sent away, and from what Jack had heard, his family never visited him.

Besides, Jack wanted to talk to Parker about it before anyone else. But his father and Parker had not yet returned from their trip. Every time he asked his mother where they were, all she said was that the masonry job was taking far longer than expected, and, "They will be home when the job is done."

With a beast roaming the woods, almost everyone in Ballylesson spent their days inside. The men still worked their farms, but they kept an ax with them at all times. The women only went out if they needed to pick up food from O'flannigan's, Ballylesson's general store. And even then, most were accompanied by at least one ax-hefting man. For the time being at least, all of Ballylesson was living in fear.

With Mrs. Dumphry nowhere to be found and the beast in the woods, Minister McCarty had canceled school for the "foreseeable future." Jack wasn't upset about the school closing; he wasn't sure he ever wanted to go back to the schoolhouse. What if that strange map was still there?

A few days after Jack's experience with the Shadowfog, Doctor Falvey stopped by the house. Jack, Alexia, and his mother were having breakfast in the kitchen. Jack's mother told Doctor Falvey about the lion. As he listened to the story, the doctor began to grin. When it was finished, he shook his head, chuckling to himself.

"Ah, these wee children do come up with the most delightful stories." He winked at Jack's mother. "I'm surprised at you, Megan, that you would believe the fancies of an orphan girl."

Before he could say another word, Alexia had grabbed a ceramic jug of milk and hurled it across the kitchen. The jug slammed into the doctor's chest, spilling warm milk down his coat and all over the floor.

"I am not an orphan, and I am not a child!" Alexia seethed.

Jack watched in wide-eyed wonder to see what his mother would do. She just looked at Alexia for a moment, clearly taken aback. Doctor Falvey was sputtering and more than a little angry as he tried unsuccessfully to wipe the milk from his coat.

Jack's mother grabbed a towel and handed it to the doctor. "Alexia," she said sternly, "we don't throw things at people when we disagree with them."

Fire flashed in Alexia's eyes, but when she looked at Jack's mother, she nodded sharply. Without a word she stalked from the kitchen. Both Jack and Doctor Falvey watched her go with a look of incredulity.

"And you, Patrick Falvey," Jack's mother said, "might want to work on your manners as well."

Doctor Falvey shook his head angrily. "That girl almost killed me, and you tell me to mind my manners?"

Jack's mother let the doctor's comment pass, and instead reminded him of the circus fire from a week earlier. "Everyone keeps talking about this beast in the woods. What else do you think it is, if not a lion?"

Doctor Falvey grudgingly agreed it was "possible that a lion was roaming the woods of Ballylesson." After admitting this, he stalked out of the house.

He paused on the porch, turned back, and said, "If there is a lion in these woods, we'll get him. We'll hang the beast's hide in the center of town for everyone to see."

Jack and his mother both turned to see if Alexia was there. There would be no stopping her if she'd heard. Fortunately for Doctor Falvey, Alexia was nowhere to be found.

Every day contained at least one unbelievable outburst from Alexia. And with each eruption, Jack's mother gave her new instructions. "Alexia," she would say in a firm, yet loving voice, "you shouldn't punch or kick people." Or, "Alexia, it's not nice to scream at someone just because you don't like them." Or, "Alexia, my dear. You really shouldn't threaten to feed people to lions. It's better to sit and talk things through when someone does something you don't like."

Besides Alexia's constant craziness, her table manners were absolutely dreadful. She slurped her food, rarely said "thank you," and used her hands as often as her fork or spoon. If a piece of meat needed to be cut, she was just as likely to grab it with her fingers and tear at it with her teeth as she was to pick up a knife and fork.

In these moments, Jack would give his mother a disbelieving look. Yet his mother would say nothing of it. And more than once she had joined Alexia and began eating with her hands as well! The whole thing confused Jack.

He couldn't wait for his brother to return. He needed to talk to someone about it all. He never quite knew what to say to Alexia, so for the moment, he decided to say nothing. Any time they found themselves it the same room, Jack quickly found a reason to be elsewhere. Only at meals did they spend any time together. And other than when he'd asked her to pass the potatoes, not a word had passed between them.

Except for the fact that his father and brother had been away far too long and they had a crazy girl living with them, except for the fact that the town of Ballylesson was still living in fear of the beast in the woods, and except for his school being closed, life began to once again feel normal. It wasn't the normal Jack was used to, but even insanity, if experienced long enough, can start to feel like a certain kind of normal.

After waiting another five days for Parker to return, Jack began to feel as if he would explode if he didn't talk to someone. Late on the evening of the fifth night, he walked into the kitchen to find his mother washing up. Alexia had gone up to her room a few minutes earlier.

"Mother, I need to tell you something," Jack said fearfully.

"I know," she answered with a smile. "It's been obvious something has been on your mind for days now. But I knew you would tell me when you were good and ready. Come, let's go out to the yard and talk there." She held out her hand and waited for Jack to take it.

Once outside, his mother lay on the grass and patted the ground next to her. "Come, my boy. Lie down and tell me what's been on your mind."

Jack took his position in the grass, then looked up to see a perfectly clear sky filled with thousands of stars. Drawing a deep breath, he began telling his mother about the voice in the fire and the dark fog. He told her about the strange map and the other Jack. He spoke until his throat was hoarse and he could think of nothing more to tell her.

When he finished, his mother stayed silent for a long time. Jack began to fear that maybe she thought he'd gone mad. *Will she send me to the asylum like Ethan Wild?* he wondered. Yet when she finally spoke, her voice was calm and loving.

"I am glad you told me, Jack. This was far too much for a boy your age to carry on his own." She paused, then asked, "Have I ever told you about the day you were born?"

"I don't think so," he said, wondering at the seeming change of subject.

"You were not the only thing born that day." She smiled and pointed toward the night sky. "Do you see that star, the one that's surrounded by the perfect circle of stars?"

Jack scanned the sky and found where she was pointing. "Yes, I see it."

"Well, that star was also born on the same day. It exploded into being in the exact moment that you were born. The constellation is called 'The Lion's Eye,' and your star is at the center of it. Before you were born, the center of the eye was dark."

Jack stared at the star in wonder. He could see it clearly. It was very bright and surrounded by a circle of seven slightly fainter stars. "Mother, are there not two stars in the center of the circle?" He squinted, trying to get a better look.

His mother grinned. "You have very keen eyes, my Jacksie. There are few on earth that could differentiate between the two. But you are correct; the two stars are side by side and very close together. Yet it is not the stars that are special; they are merely signs that point us toward what is truly special." His mother sat up and placed Jack's head on her lap, stroking his hair lovingly.

"You are not a normal boy, Jack. Your birth was prophesied even before our world came into being. There are things you can do that no one else can. There are things you were born to do."

Jack was dumbfounded. He didn't know what to think. Was his mother as mad as he was?

"We have not told you before now because no child should have to carry such a heavy burden. But it seems the time has come." She smiled warmly. "Yet, what I have to tell you will be easier to hear when the sun is up. Besides which, Alexia will need to hear it as well."

"You want Alexia to know?"

"Yes, because Alexia is also special. The two of you are unlike any two people who have ever lived before. But let us talk more in the morning when we are all together. I love you, Jack. And I have never been more proud of you. Now off to bed, my boy. It's late and the morning will come before you know it." She pulled him close and kissed his cheek.

Chapter 12

THE STRANGER

Alexia lay in bed staring at the ceiling. Warm sunlight shone through her bedroom window, casting the shadow of a nearby oak on the wall. Mrs. Staples had told her this was Parker's room. Parker was the woman's oldest son who was away with his father. "But," she'd said, "Parker can share a room with Jack when he gets home. The room is yours, if you want it."

She still couldn't believe it. She was in a real bed in her very own bedroom, and she was staying with a family! The thought was almost too much to bear. She hadn't slept in a real bed since her fifth birthday. As often as not in those first few years, Alexia had awakened to find herself lying on the topmost branches of a nearby tree or on the peak of the tallest roof. The first few times this happened, it had taken her many hours to climb down. Yet after a few months of waking up in trees or on rooftops, she'd begun feeling quite comfortable. Her father had been right. She was Alexia Dreager, the Ally Goat, and she could climb anything.

One day Alexia had decided she wanted to be brave like her mother and father. It had been a good day. She'd stood on the bow of a large birch tree and stepped off, letting herself fall for a moment before grabbing a branch. It was so easy! Hanging by one arm, she'd laughed. If someone had seen her hanging high up in the tree, they'd have thought she'd lost her senses. If they'd seen what she did next, they would have been sure of it.

Alexia swung her body around so the top of her head faced the ground, then straightened her legs and let go. She closed her eyes and visualized the branches below. Even as she fell, she began to laugh. It was so much fun! At the last moment she reached out and grabbed a branch near the bottom and, using the momentum of the fall, swung her body all the way around it. Then with the momentum she had gained, she let go of the branch and flew, tucking her knees into her chest and doing a backward somersault. She landed on the ground with her hands held high. It had been a truly wonderful day.

However, since the first night Alexia had fallen asleep in Mrs. Staples's house, she'd awoken in her bed every morning. She smiled again at the thought, *her bed*. Megan Staples had told her, "You will always have a home with us."

"A home," Alexia whispered. The word felt strange on her tongue. For years she'd dreamed of having a real home, of belonging to someone. But she never expected it to happen. And even better than a home, Megan Staples had given her the best gift she'd received since her fifth birthday.

As she lay in bed, a dark cloud began forming in the clear morning sky just outside her window. Yet Alexia was not paying attention to the cloud; instead she was remembering her first morning with Megan Staples. Had it only been six days ago? Alexia had woken up to find her cloak, sling, and brand-new clothes lying on top of the dresser. Megan had sewn her a deep purple blouse with six pearl buttons down the front. On the chest, golden thread formed an intricate pattern of a great bird with its wings outstretched across the shoulders. It really was quite beautiful.

It was on this first morning within the Staples house when Alexia made her decision to stay. She hadn't been sure when she'd awoken, but it was the conversation with Megan in the kitchen that made up her mind. Alexia grinned at the memory.

SIX DAYS EARLIER

"Good morning, Alexia. I hope you slept well." Megan Staples wore a bright yellow apron, and her sleeves were rolled up past the elbows. Her lip was split, and her left eye was black and blue. Besides that, her arms were covered in scratches. All of the wounds had come from

Alexia, yet you never would know it by the way Megan behaved. Her smile was true and inviting. "I made some breakfast, if you are hungry," she said. "I'm so glad the clothes fit! I wasn't sure I'd gotten the measurements right."

Alexia blushed. "I was just getting ready to leave," she said stubbornly, "but I guess I'll eat something before I go."

Megan beamed as if Alexia had just given her the best gift in the world. "Oh, that's such great news! Come and wash your hands and we'll have breakfast together!" She turned and took her own advice, scrubbing her hands with a thick bar of soap.

Alexia tried to pull herself together. Why hadn't she demanded the woman tell her everything? Why did she say she would stay for breakfast? She needed to get into the woods and find Killer before he did something stupid. Yet when she looked at the counter, she saw the food. There were eggs, bacon, freshly baked bread, porridge, fresh fruit, and hot tea.

Megan followed her look and smiled. "I wasn't sure what you liked, so I decided to give you a few options."

The food took Alexia's breath away. Forgetting all about her questions, she walked to the table and sat down. She ignored the silverware, picked up three pieces of bacon, and stuffed them into her mouth. She'd barely chewed them before slurping a spoonful of porridge followed by a full glass of milk that dribbled down her chin. She didn't look up from her food until she'd grabbed a fried egg with her fingers. As the yolk dripped to her elbow, she saw Megan watching her with wide eyes.

Alexia worried she had done something wrong. But Megan merely smiled, placed her knife and fork on the table, and picked up an egg with her fingers, taking a large bite. With yolk dripping from her chin, she began to laugh.

When Megan laughed, so did Alexia. She couldn't help it; the sight of the woman eating with her hands was truly funny. "Ah, my girl, I'd forgotten how much fun it is to break a rule every now and again. Thank you for reminding me."

After a moment, Megan spoke in a serious tone. "Alexia, I know you want to leave, and I promise I would never try to keep you here against your will. But if you stay, I will be so very happy, even if you decide to stay for only a few days."

Alexia didn't know what to say. She was silent for a moment as she turned to stare out the window. When she finally met Megan's eyes, she asked the only question that seemed to matter.

"How do you know my name?"

Megan stayed quiet a long time. When she spoke, tears leaked from her eyes once more. "I read the inscription sewn into your cloak. I wasn't trying to pry; I saw it while I was cleaning it for you."

Alexia was confused. What was the woman talking about? There was nothing sewn into her cloak. Before it had been transformed into a cloak, it had been a dress, and in one form or another, she'd been wearing it nearly every day since her fifth birthday. She would know if something was there. Alexia was about to say as much when Megan saw the confusion on her face, stood up, and walked over. She reached out her hand and waited. Feeling as if she were in a dream, Alexia took off her cloak and handed it to her.

She watched as Megan turned her inside pocket inside out. And there, in golden thread at the bottom of the pocket was an inscription that had been sewn in.

My darling Alexia. You bring light into my world. When you've lost your way and your heart grows cold, the memory of love will guide you home.

Alexia was dumbfounded. How had she never seen this before? She'd used the pocket often. This was where she carried the extra stones for her sling. It's true she'd never been very clean and had rarely washed the cloak over the years, but still, how had she missed it?

Megan saw the shock in her eyes. "It's easy to be blind to what we think is not there." Her words were not chiding, but kind. Once again, Alexia found tears wetting her cheeks as she ran her fingers over the inscription again and again. Megan turned and began wiping one of the counters.

You bring light into my world. Alexia silently read the words again. After so many years, to receive a message from her mother was almost unbelievable.

"If it's okay," Alexia said, "I would like to stay here. At least for a little while."

Megan didn't turn right away. She breathed in heavily and wiped fresh tears from her eyes. Then she turned and beamed at Alexia. "This is your house now, and you will never be asked to leave."

She walked over and gave Alexia a big hug, then sat down and poured tea. As she was pouring, Alexia spoke in a sullen voice. "I'm sorry about hitting you. I didn't ... I don't ...," she said, unsure of what to say.

"You have nothing to apologize for. Although, I must admit if I'd known how strong you are, I might have tried to block a few more of those punches!" She chuckled.

Alexia laughed as well. She didn't know what to make of the woman, but she was sure she liked her very much.

A short while later, both women turned to look toward the sound of someone running down the stairs. A voice called out, "Mother, you won't believe it. Last night, I dreamed—" A skinny boy sprinted into the room. The instant their eyes met, Alexia was enraged. The boy lived here?

SIX DAYS LATER

As she lay in bed, Alexia smiled at the memory. Her days with Megan Staples had been magical. Everything was as perfect as it could be. The only real rule Megan had given her was to be home before dark. And though Alexia pretended not to like the rule, if she was being honest, she liked it very much. For eight years she'd had no one to look after her. The fact that someone actually cared where she was and what she was doing made her feel warm inside.

There were, of course, a few problems every now and then, but they were relatively minor in Alexia's mind. Megan didn't want her to throw things or fight or hurt people in general. And screaming and yelling never impressed her. Besides these minor shortcomings, Megan Staples was quite definitely the nicest and wisest woman Alexia had ever met, besides her mother, of course.

Megan's son Jack, on the other hand, was as skinny as a rail and seemed to be afraid of everything. Alexia wasn't sure what to think of him just yet. For now, she'd decided it was best not to speak to him at all.

As she lay in bed, Alexia began to cry. Her tears weren't because she was sad, but because she was so very happy. After so many years alone, she finally had a home. She had someone to belong to. Jumping out of bed, she decided today would be the day she would ask Megan if she could stay here permanently. She imagined Megan would probably be so excited she might even cook Alexia's favorite meal.

As she finished getting dressed, Alexia saw the black clouds gathering just outside her bedroom window.

Boom!

She jumped. Although a bright light had flashed outside, she was sure it hadn't been lightning, and the boom was not thunder. She'd spent many a night sleeping out in thunderstorms, and whatever that sound had been, it was not caused by weather. And whatever that slithering darkness was, it was no cloud.

With fear gripping her heart, Alexia walked slowly to the window. A wall of roiling darkness rose from the front yard high into the morning sky. From somewhere deep within, a flash of light exploded again, and when it did, she saw Megan Staples standing in the midst of it. Her arms were spread wide, and a pool of white light surrounded her. In front of Megan was a being with eyes of fire and a sickly white cloak. As the light faded, Megan once again disappeared inside the mass of slithering shadows.

Sprinting out of her room and down the stairs, Alexia barely noticed the eggs and strawberries lying on the floor, and she ran right over the crumpled apron by the front door. The moment she opened the door, there was another explosion.

Boom!

A great wind slammed into Alexia, knocking her flat on her back on the entryway floor. For a moment, her ears rang and the world spun. As her head began to clear, Alexia rose to a sitting position. Confused, she looked outside to see the sun shining in a cloudless sky. Hadn't it been dark just a moment earlier? Her eyes focused as she stood and leaned heavily against the doorframe. And then she saw her.

Alexia stumbled off the porch and over to Megan, who was lying on her back on a sea of grass. Dropping to her knees, she grabbed Megan's hand in hers. She was alive but incredibly pale, and she was trying to say something, yet struggling to speak. Alexia knelt and placed her ear to Megan's lips, desperate to help, to hear her words.

"I am sorry, my girl. I wanted to tell you about … about everything. Thought we had … more time." Megan convulsed in pain, yet Alexia couldn't find any injuries on her body. "You are special. You both are …" She coughed again as pain wracked her body. "The Assassin wants to steal you away, but he is evil! I wanted more time." Tears leaked from the corners of her eyes. "I love you, my girl … always have …" With one final convulsion, Megan Staples exhaled a long, slow breath, and the light faded from her eyes. Once again, Alexia Dreager's world stopped.

A few minutes later, Jack Staples also ran out the front door. When he did, Alexia barely noticed him. She was sitting next to Megan's body, holding her hand and rubbing it softly. She had shed no tears. She'd not had a single thought. She just sat and held Megan's hand in hers.

When Jack screamed the first time, she ignored him. Only when he was standing over her, screaming again, did she look up.

I wonder if this is how I looked when my parents died? she wondered numbly. When Jack fell to his knees, she watched him curiously. As he collapsed on top of his mother, unable to fill his lungs due to the shock he was feeling, she didn't move. Alexia knew there was nothing that could be done to help at a time like this.

Almost an hour later, Jack and Alexia hadn't moved. And though Alexia's eyes were open and there was nothing stuffed in her ears, she neither saw nor heard anything. After a moment she realized they were no longer alone. A stranger had arrived from somewhere and was kneeling over Jack and Megan. The stranger had to be the oldest woman Alexia had ever seen. She had long gray hair pulled up in a large bun and wrinkly skin with sunken eyes. Alexia watched as the old woman lifted Jack's limp body off of Megan Staples. Placing two fingers to his neck, the woman checked to see if he was alive. Next, she bent over Megan and did the same.

"Stand up, child. We haven't much time," the old woman said in a brusque tone.

Alexia's head felt as though it were stuffed with wool. She could barely make out what the woman was saying.

"I am not accustomed to having to say things twice. My name is Mrs. Dumphry and I expect you to listen. If you want to stay alive, you will do as I say. And if you want to help Megan Staples, you will do it quickly. The Oriax have come, and there's no time to dally."

Chapter 13

WHEN EVERYTHING CHANGES

Boom! Jack's eyes shot open as thunder roared from somewhere outside his window. Pulling the covers up past his nose, he stared out his bedroom window at the darkening sky. Something about the boiling clouds terrified him.

He wasn't sure, but he thought it must be morning. When a second clap of thunder rattled the windows, Jack squeezed his eyes shut, pulling the covers over his head. He was much too afraid to go and look out the window.

He lay under the covers feeling like a foolish child. *You're too old to be afraid of the dark!* he berated himself. When he pulled the covers down from his head, he saw that outside the sky was blue and the sun shone brightly. *Maybe it was a dream,* he thought as he stepped from his bed and quickly dressed. Still too nervous to look out the window, Jack went in search of his mother.

When he reached the bottom of the stairs, he saw her apron lying crumpled on the floor next to the open front door. Still not wanting to look outside, he walked toward the kitchen and stepped on a broken piece of crockery. His mother's two favorite mixing bowls lay shattered on the floor with five broken eggs and a number of strawberries scattered nearby.

Jack ran into the kitchen. The moment he entered, he coughed at the smoke filling the air. He quickly spotted a frying pan filled with burning bacon, sizzling on the stove. His mother was nowhere in sight.

As he ran to the next room, fear formed a knot in his belly. "Mother, where are you?" There was no answer. He darted up the stairs and into his parents' bedroom, finding it empty. He walked to the window, and the foreboding grew stronger. At first he wasn't sure what he was seeing. His mother was lying on the ground in the font yard with Alexia sitting beside her.

Terror gripped him as he lumbered out of the room and down the stairs. When he darted out the front door, he stopped.

"Mother." Jack's voice was hesitant. "Mother, what's wrong?" His throat tightened.

Alexia must have known he was there. She must have heard him speaking, but she didn't move. Jack stepped forward. "Mother!" he screamed. "Talk to me! What's going on?"

Darkness pushed at the edges of his vision, but he forced it away, making himself take another step. His mother was very pale, and her eyes stared unblinking at the sky.

"Why is she just lying there?" he screamed.

Alexia wore a blank expression as she gently rubbed his mother's hand. She was staring out at the forest, but didn't seem to be looking at anything in particular. Jack couldn't breathe. Alexia blinked and looked up at him as if she were only now noticing he was there. Still she didn't say a word.

The darkness pushed in harder as the world began to spin. He dropped to his knees. No matter how hard he tried, he couldn't fill his lungs. As he gasped for breath, somewhere in the distance Jack heard the ringing of bells.

Overwhelmed with grief, he collapsed and landed on top of his mother. The last thing he remembered was the distinct sensation of flying backward, high into the air.

Jack stood in the upstairs hallway listening to the bells. Abruptly, he realized he wasn't breathing. Dropping to his knees, he gasped, feeling as if someone had punched him in the gut. Something was wrong. Something terrible had just happened, but what? He wracked his brain, trying to remember. Struggling to his feet, he opened his bedroom door and looked out the window with a sense of dread. Jack was starting to feel sick. It was snowing hard, and the world was covered in a thick sheet of white. Yet Jack didn't see the snow or the man and two boys building a very large snowman in the front yard. Instead, he saw his mother's body lying on a sea of green grass. She wasn't really there, but as he looked, he could see her in his mind's eye, and he remembered.

"Mother!" he screamed as he bolted from the room. "Mother, where are you?" Sprinting through the hallway and down the stairs, he screamed again, "Mother!" As he entered the kitchen, he was surprised to find his mother with her sleeves rolled and flour covering her arms up to the elbows.

"You're alive!" he exclaimed, wrapping her in a hug.

"Jack, what is it?" She was breathless. "Why are you screaming? What's happened?"

Jack felt tears in his eyes, and his head swam dizzily. "What's happening?" he asked. "You died. You ... you were dead! You were outside on the ground. Please, tell me what's going on. Alexia was there, and she ..."

His mother let go of his hands and took a step back, a look of pain and disbelief crossing her face. "What did you say?"

"You were dead. You were lying on the ground, and you were—"

"Not that!" she said, cutting him off. "Who was there, Jack?" She stepped forward and grabbed him by the shoulders. "Who did you say was beside me?"

"Alexia was there. She found you first. I don't know what happened, but I ..."

The blood drained from his mother's face, and she whispered, "I need to sit down." She lowered herself to the kitchen floor.

"Mother, what's happening?"

His mother reached out. Jack sank down next to her, enfolded in her arms. "Oh, my Jacksie, it's going to be okay. Everything is going to be okay. I need you to tell me everything, and I need you to do it right now. You are—" She stopped as if unsure what to say. "You are dreaming, and you will wake any minute now. But tell me everything you know about Alexia."

Jack pushed his mother away angrily. "She doesn't matter!" he said. "Didn't you hear me? You died! And if this is just a dream, then you're dead, and there's nothing I can do about it!"

"Listen to me. I'm sorry, but I haven't been fully honest with you. This is …" She paused again, looking for the right words. "It's more than a dream. I'm not supposed to tell you, but maybe it's time you found out."

Just then the front door slammed open. Jack's father called out, "We're back! And ready for some of Mom's famous hot chocolate."

His mother looked toward the sound of his father's voice. "We need to hide you," she whispered. Moving quickly, she took Jack by the shoulders and led him to the back entry.

"Where are we going?"

"I need you to stay quiet. We're running out of time, and I can't let the boys see you." As his mother opened the back door, Jack saw that the snowfall was much heavier now. The snow was so deep it reached his knees.

"Megan," Jack's father called again. "Where are you? You've got to come see the size of this snowman. It's twice as tall as Parker and three times bigger than Jack!"

Jack's head was swimming as his mother pushed him out into the snow. The cold was intense, and wind whipped at his shirt, making him shiver. His bare feet turned to icicles. After closing the door behind them, she quickly knelt and held his face in her hands.

"Listen to me, Jack. You can control it. It's just like any dream. You are in control. You can change things. Not completely, but you can shift them." She spread her hands, gesturing toward the world around them. "But you must concentrate! I couldn't tell you earlier because it was too dangerous, but it's time you learned."

"What are you talking about? What do you mean 'control it'?" Jack had to shout to be heard over the wind. "Mother, haven't you been listening? You are dead! You died in the front yard! I found your body."

"That's enough!" she said angrily. "Don't say another word about it."

Fresh tears sprang to his eyes; the wind threatened to turn them into icicles too. He was confused and hurt that his mother wouldn't listen to him.

"I am sorry," she said as she scooped him up and pulled him close. He hugged her as tightly as he could, and when she hugged him back, he thought his ribs might crack, but he didn't care.

His mother was also crying now. Pulling him even closer, she whispered into his ear. "I need to ask you to do something for me. I need you to look after Alexia. If she is truly alive, you take care of each other. The two of you must stay together no matter what happens!" His mother kissed him on the forehead before continuing. "And if you haven't met her yet, you will soon meet Elion. Know that you can trust her above all."

Jack had no idea what his mother was talking about, but he nodded anyway.

"What I must ask you next will be much harder. But when the time comes, I need you to let me go." She held his face in both hands. "You cannot fix everything. No matter how hard you try, you can't save everyone."

"No! I won't do it!" Jack told her. He didn't care what she said; he wasn't willing to let her die.

"Please, Jack!" she pleaded. "You must promise me."

As the ringing of bells sounded once again, Jack exploded out of his mother's arms, flying backward through the air.

Disoriented and confused, Jack opened his eyes and began to scream. His leg burned like fire. When he looked down, he saw a beast unlike anything he'd seen before. It had blood-red eyes and two rows of razor-sharp fangs in its black snout. And the terrifying beast had bitten down hard on his leg.

Chapter 14

THE ORIAX

"I am not accustomed to saying things twice. My name is Mrs. Dumphry, and I expect you to listen. If you want to stay alive, you will do as I say. And if you want to help Megan Staples, you will do it quickly. The Oriax have come. There's no time to dally."

Alexia stared at Mrs. Dumphry. *Who is this old woman, and what is she going on about?* Alexia's thoughts were about to form into words when something howled from deep in the forest. It was unlike anything she'd heard before, followed by a shriek that was immediately followed by a great gurgling hiss.

"Stand up!" Mrs. Dumphry's voice held such a note of authority that Alexia found herself standing without thinking.

"Pick up the boy and follow me." Mrs. Dumphry began walking toward the house.

"We can't just leave her." Alexia felt numb as she motioned toward Megan Staples.

"If you want to help Megan, then you must come with me, now!" Mrs. Dumphry said. "The Oriax don't care about her; it's the two of you they're after."

More beastly cries sounded from the forest. There were howls, gurgles, shrieks, hisses, and roars. They were coming closer by the second, yet Alexia barely heard. Could it be true? Could Megan Staples really be alive? If listening to the old woman meant saving Megan, Alexia would do anything she asked.

Placing Jack on her back, Alexia followed behind Mrs. Dumphry. When another roar sounded, closer this time, she turned to see two beasts surge out of the forest. Alexia had traveled with the circus long enough to know almost every kind of animal, but the creatures running toward her now were unlike anything she'd seen before.

One of the beasts had the head of a wolf but was as big as a horse. And its neck was long and covered in the shiny black scales of a serpent. Alexia couldn't see clearly, but she thought its body was also different. Scurrying beside it was another beast with the head of a bear and the body of some sort of lizard.

A moment later, another beast leaped from the forest. This one had the head and shoulders of a rat and the body of a frog. The creature bounded high into the air, covering a huge amount of ground with each jump. The beasts' only similarities were their blood-red eyes, their large size, and their fangs that gleamed in the morning light.

"Run, you foolish girl!" Mrs. Dumphry's voice was urgent. Alexia hadn't realized she'd stopped. As she turned to run, another beast slithered out of the woods. And though she ran as fast as she could, with Jack on her back she felt as though she were running through mud.

Alexia ran toward the old woman who was now standing on the porch with her arms raised and palms outstretched. She couldn't tell for sure, but she thought Mrs. Dumphry's hands were beginning to change color. Suddenly another hooded figure stalked out from behind the house. He had a bow in hand and an arrow nocked.

"Get down!" he screamed as he loosed an arrow that flew straight at Alexia. She dropped to the ground, and the missile whizzed past, nicking her ear. Though she didn't see what happened next, Alexia felt a flash of heat pass over her.

Thwang. Another arrow flew overhead. She tried to scramble to her feet, but Jack was on top of her, pinning her down. She looked back to see the beast with the wolf's head and snake's neck scrambling toward her. An arrow sprouted from its snout, but it barely seemed to notice.

The hellish beast moved with a viper's speed as it whipped its head back and sprang forward. Alexia moved her feet at the last second, but the beast's fangs closed around Jack's leg. She kicked it hard in the snout as Jack's eyes shot open and he began to scream. *Thwang!* A second arrow struck the beast between the eyes, killing it instantly.

"You cut that too close, Wild." Mrs. Dumphry glanced back at the hooded stranger as she rushed over to Jack. Grabbing the beast's heavy head from his leg, she shoved it aside. Jack was wide-eyed as he looked from his ruined leg to Mrs. Dumphry.

"P-please, help me. It ... it burns. Please!" Jack stammered, his voice full of pain.

Mrs. Dumphry quickly lifted Jack to a sitting position and slugged him hard in the face, knocking him out.

"What are you doing?" Alexia screamed.

Without responding, the old woman produced a small vial of dark liquid. After uncorking it, she poured it over Jack's wounds. As the liquid touched his leg, it began to smoke and hiss as if landing on a frying pan.

"What did you do to him?" Alexia asked.

"I saved his life," Mrs. Dumphry snapped as the last drops fell from the vial. "At least for now. Few survive the bite of an Oriax. If the child had remained conscious, he wouldn't have stayed still long enough for me to help him."

Alexia's eyes shifted between the four dead beasts in front of her. Two of them had arrows sprouting between their eyes, and the other two had somehow been burned to death. How did that happen? The beast that had bitten Jack had the scaled neck of a snake, a wolf's head, and the body and legs of a goat. The others were equally strange, each a blend of mammal and reptile. Yet none of them looked awkward, but seemed natural as skin blended into fur or scale. The only similarities between them were their blood-red eyes and two rows of razor-sharp fangs.

As Alexia studied the stranger who'd loosed the arrows, she was surprised to see a boy. He was close to her age with dirty-blond curls sprouting at every angle, and his eyes were more orange than brown. When he met Alexia's stare, he blushed, immediately shifting his gaze back to the forest.

"I'm sorry I was late," the boy said to Mrs. Dumphry, "but I was busy trying to stay alive. There was a Shadule in the center of town."

Mrs. Dumphry's head whipped around in shock. "You're sure?"

"I'm sure ..." The boy hesitated. "I don't understand it, and I don't know how, but the Shadule was dead. I found the creature lying headless in O'flannigans."

Mrs. Dumphry exhaled heavily, looking in the direction of Ballylesson. "What could have killed a Shadule? And why?" she whispered. After a moment, she shook her head and turned to the boy. "We need a wagon and horses."

"Already done," the boy said, motioning toward the back of the house.

Alexia hated being ignored almost as much as she hated being afraid. "Someone is going to tell me what's going on," she demanded. "What happened to Megan Staples? Can you help her? And what are those beasts?"

"Child, do you consider yourself my equal?" the old woman asked.

Alexia was confused by the question.

"For I do not consider myself your playmate, nor do I wish to be," Mrs. Dumphry continued. "A sparrow and a hawk may both be birds, but they fly at very different heights. I understand you have questions, and I plan to answer many once we are safely away, but right now we are leaving."

"You think I'm going anywhere with you?" Alexia stomped her foot. "I'd like to see you make me!"

"Make you?" Mrs. Dumphry sounded perplexed. "Behind you are four dead Oriax. I would guess there hasn't been an Oriax in these parts for thousands of years. On my way here I passed an entire pack of the beasts, all coming in this direction. And if you walk into Ballylesson, you will find that much of it is burning or already destroyed." Mrs. Dumphry glanced at the large plumes of smoke rising from the direction of the town. "And Wild now tells us there is also a dead Shadule. A Shadule is infinitely more deadly than an Oriax and almost impossible to kill. If it is dead, something far worse lurks nearby."

Mrs. Dumphry took a slow step toward Alexia. "This evil has come here for you, child. It hunts you and the boy," she said, glancing at Jack. "Stay, if you like, but know this: if you do, you will die or be captured before the sun sets. Or, you may come with me. I cannot promise to keep you alive, but I promise you will at least live longer."

"You said you could help her," Alexia insisted, motioning to Megan. She didn't know what the old woman was talking about, but as she looked toward Megan, it seemed the only thing to say. "You said if I come with you, she would be all right."

"If you come with me, I promise to do all I can for Megan Staples."

Just then, a pudgy boy peeked out from behind the house. He was as white as a bedsheet and had a bandage wrapped around his forehead, covering the top half of his eyes. He walked on unsteady legs and looked as if he were trying to wake from a bad dream. Even with the bandage, he squinted, as if the sun were too bright.

"Hello! Are you still there? Who's talking?" His voice quavered.

"I told you not to bring anyone." Mrs. Dumphry's voice, directed at the boy she called Wild, was icy. "You were to check for these two, then meet me here."

Wild dropped his eyes, but when he spoke, there was stubbornness in his voice. "Something bad happened in Ballylesson. O'flannigans has been destroyed, and there was a battle of some sort in the street. Besides the Shadule, there were seven dead Oriax." When he met Mrs. Dumphry's eyes, his face became hard. "I couldn't just leave him there. I found him stumbling like a newborn lamb. Look at him! He is one of the Awakened now. His scales have fallen off."

Mrs. Dumphry's eyes were as cold as the grave. "Arthur Greaves," she called out. The boy turned to face her, one hand shielding his eyes. "You had better not slow us down."

Arthur paled even more. "Mrs. Dumphry, is that you? What's happening? Do you know where my mother is?"

Mrs. Dumphry gave Arthur a withering glance, then looked at Wild. "He's your responsibility. Put Megan in the house, then meet us at the wagon. We leave now."

"You don't mean to bring her with us?" Alexia was furious.

"She is in no state to travel. The only way to keep anyone in this town safe is to get you and Jack away from here as soon as possible."

"You have to—"

"Child," Mrs. Dumphry said, cutting her off. "You are a sapling standing before an avalanche. There is no winning right now."

When Alexia met the old woman's eyes, she took an involuntary step back. She had to physically unstick her tongue from the roof of her mouth.

The boy with the bow and arrows—Wild—walked toward Alexia and awkwardly extended his hand. "My name is Ethan Wild, but the Awakened just call me Wild. I've been looking forward to meeting you."

Alexia was thankful for the opportunity to turn away from Mrs. Dumphry's gaze. She glanced at Wild's extended hand, rolled her eyes, and stalked toward the wagon.

Chapter 15

THE BATTLE BEGINS

In a matter of minutes, Arthur, Alexia, and Jack were in the back of a covered wagon. The moment they had climbed in, Mrs. Dumphry whispered sharply, "Do not make a sound, or we will all die today." Without another word, she closed the wagon's cover and tied it shut. Inside it was black as pitch.

Arthur sat in the darkness with his knees pulled to his chest and his palms placed hard against his eyes. He could hear Jack's labored breathing coming from the direction of his feet. And though he couldn't see Alexia, he could hear her breathing from the opposite bench.

Arthur hadn't seen Alexia since a week earlier when Mrs. Dumphry had knocked her out with the rock. Yet he'd heard stories about her. All of Ballylesson had been talking about "the wild girl" living with the Staples. Though he hadn't been able to see her clearly when he was outside, he'd recognized her voice.

For a very long time, the only sound was the creaking of the wagon wheels, the steady plodding of the horses, and the breathing of the three children. Every now and then the wagon stopped. When it did, Arthur held his breath until it lurched forward again.

He didn't understand it, but something was wrong with his eyes. The pain was starting to subside, but even the smallest amount of light made him squint terribly. He was glad Mrs. Dumphry had tied the back of the wagon shut; the light outside was piercing. But he didn't want to think about the light. He didn't want to think about any of it.

Finally, when he could stand the silence no longer, he whispered, "What happened to Jack?"

A minute passed before Alexia spoke, but when she did, it wasn't to answer Arthur's question. "Is it true what she said? Was the town destroyed?"

This time it was Arthur's turn to stay silent. He'd been trying not to think about what happened in Ballylesson. When he finally spoke, his voice shook with fear.

"I was at O'flannigans with Mother," he whispered. "We were there to buy some sugar and grain, and I had to, you know"—Arthur suddenly felt embarrassed—"I had to go. So I went to the outhouse behind the store, and that's when the screaming started. I don't know, but I think most everyone in town was screaming. I wanted to run out, to see what was happening, but …" His throat caught. "But I was too afraid to move."

"When I looked through a slit in the side of the outhouse, I saw an old scabby dog. It was chasing Mrs. Wetworth, and one of the buildings across the street was on fire. Then something crashed outside. It sounded like someone was fighting. I wanted to go to Mother, but I couldn't move. I wasn't brave enough." He broke down in tears. "I heard something scream. I don't know what, but I'm sure it was evil. Don't laugh, but its voice scared me more than anything I've ever heard."

"What did it say?" Alexia whispered.

"It was begging for mercy, like it was afraid or something. It said, 'Spare me!' and then …" Arthur began to shake. "And then a black sword pierced through the outhouse door; it nearly took my head off! And whoever or whatever had been begging was suddenly quiet."

"I don't understand. You're saying the evil voice was begging for mercy?" Alexia asked.

"Yes. And that's what I've been wondering. If it really was evil, then whatever it was afraid of must have been far worse, right?" Arthur didn't wait for Alexia to respond. "When I finally left the outhouse, I saw someone. It was a pale, bony man who was covered in sores and dressed in rags." Arthur swallowed, continuing in a harsh whisper. "He was lying on the ground, and I'm not sure, but I think he was dead. And I don't know why, but just then my eyes started to burn like fire, and for just a moment, it wasn't a man lying on the ground but a monster. I called for my mother, but she didn't answer." Arthur's entire body began to tremble. "I don't know if she was still in the store because I couldn't see anything. My eyes were hurting so badly. I don't know where she is or if she's even …," Arthur trailed off.

After a moment he continued. "That's when the boy walked in and found me. Do—" Arthur's throat tightened. "Do you think they're dead—my mother and father and the rest of the town?"

"I don't know," Alexia whispered. "I don't know what's happening, but whatever it is, I don't think we can trust the old woman. Those beasts didn't arrive until she did."

"Mrs. Dumphry?" Arthur said in surprise. "She's been here forever. She's my teacher—Jack's and mine. Some people say she's over two hundred years old."

"Don't be stupid," Alexia whispered. "No one is that old."

"I didn't say I believed it," Arthur whispered back, slightly hurt. "I've just heard people say it. Besides, why wouldn't we trust her? Didn't she kill those beasts?"

Before Alexia could respond, the wagon stopped again. Arthur's eyes followed the sounds of someone walking around to the back. After a moment, the cover was pulled aside to reveal soft moonlight shining in. Arthur was amazed. They'd spent most of the day in the back of the wagon and ridden well into the night. Although his eyes were beginning to feel better, he still squinted at the brightness of the moon.

"There is evil nearby," Mrs. Dumphry whispered. "Remain silent. The Oriax have come, and unless I miss my guess, a Shadule leads them."

Arthur wanted to ask how she knew it was near and what kind of evil it might be, but he was much too afraid to say anything.

"Girl," Mrs. Dumphry whispered. "Do you still have that sling of yours? If I remember correctly, you had some skill with it."

"How do you know about my sling?" Alexia whispered back irritably.

"Do you have it or not?"

"Yes, I have it," Alexia replied sullenly.

"Come with me and keep it at the ready."

Alexia hesitated a moment before crawling out of the wagon.

"You," Mrs. Dumphry said to Arthur, "will take the Staples boy. You will keep him quiet and remain hidden. And you will not move or make a sound, no matter what happens!"

Without another word, Mrs. Dumphry turned and walked into the night with Alexia following behind.

Arthur stood, frozen in fear. Had Mrs. Dumphry really just left him? Where was he meant to hide? When he heard a scratching sound behind him, Arthur spun and very nearly screamed. Wild stood in the wagon rubbing Jack's cloak vigorously against the cloth walls. Feeling stupid for forgetting about Wild, Arthur blushed furiously. Luckily it was too dark for the older boy to notice.

"What are you doing?" Arthur whispered.

"The Shadow Souled hunt by smell. I want to make sure they think Jack is in here," Wild said as he dropped the cloak and crouched low. "Well, are you going to help me or not?"

Arthur quickly knelt and grabbed Jack's legs. The moment his fingers touched Jack's skin, he gasped. "His leg is hot!"

"Are you a doctor now?" Wild retorted. Before Arthur could think of a response, Wild continued. "No, you are not. So why don't you let Mrs. Dumphry worry about his leg, and just do as you're told?"

Arthur felt a little hurt, but nodded and picked up the bottom half of his best friend. Jack's leg was hotter than he would have thought possible. It was only a few short steps until Arthur and Wild were standing next to a large bush. As they laid Jack on the ground,

Wild dropped to his knees and shoved him forward. When his friend disappeared, Arthur gasped again.

"Will you stay silent?" Wild whispered angrily. "Get in, and whatever you do, don't move."

As Arthur dropped to his knees, he saw a small hole that had been hollowed out beneath the bush. It wouldn't hide them completely, but unless someone was right on top of them, it should do the job. He crawled in and quickly pulled Jack close. Even though his friend was unconscious, he was still glad he was not alone in the hole.

When Wild turned to walk away, Arthur whispered after him, "Where are you going?"

Wild shot Arthur an angry look and placed his finger to his lips, making a shushing motion, then climbed into the back of the wagon and disappeared from view.

Arthur barely breathed as he searched the surrounding forest, trying to see everything at once. And though his eyes still ached, his vision was returning. Except, he was relatively certain that the shadows weren't quite so dark as they should have been. And he could see more detail than ever before. His eyes followed a small beetle crawling across the ground a few steps away. It shouldn't have been possible to see so clearly.

As the minutes passed, his fear began to subside. Besides his eyesight, nothing seemed unusual about the night. Maybe Mrs. Dumphry had been mistaken. After an hour of sitting in the hole, he was on the edge of sleep. Just as he was about to close his eyes and embrace the coming dreams, he heard a soft whoosh. Suddenly wide awake, Arthur listened intently. The sound made him think of the blacksmith bellows his father sometimes used. Each time his dad took him into Ballylesson, they had stopped by Mr. McReady's forge. His father would walk inside without saying a word. He'd grab the bellows and begin pumping in a slow, steady rhythm. Mr. McReady would look back and smile in thanks as he continued his work.

"I know it looks easy, Arthur," his father would say, "but only a man with a steady hand and sure rhythm can be master of the bellows."

When Arthur's father pumped the bellows, it made a whoosh each time the air was pushed through the small hole. He could hear the same sound now, except it was much quicker, as if the bellows were pumping furiously.

Arthur's breath caught as something dropped from high up in the sky. It landed directly between him and the wagon without making a sound. Fear swelled as a shadowed figure rose fluidly from the ground. It was hulking, with webbed wings extending from its back. As it stood, the wings began wrapping themselves around the strange creature. The wings didn't fold into its back, but rather melted into its body, becoming a sort of second skin.

Although his vision was blurred, Arthur had seen the dead beasts outside of Jack's house. Mrs. Dumphry had called them Oriax, and though they'd scared him witless, this was infinitely worse. *This must be the Shadule Mrs. Dumphry was talking about*, he thought shakily. And while he couldn't say for sure, he thought it was the same type of creature that he'd found lying headless inside O'flannigans.

The Shadule radiated evil much the same way an ice cube radiates cold. As it stood fully upright, Arthur placed his hands over Jack's mouth to quiet his breathing. The creature was directly facing them. It blended so well with the night that the only things Arthur could see clearly were the solid white slits of its eyes.

Letting its head fall back at an impossible angle, the creature began to sway and make a soft rattling sound. It moved more like a snake than a man as it sniffed the air. Keeping its feet anchored to the ground, the creature bent so that its entire body hovered just above the forest floor. It moved so fluidly that Arthur was sure it couldn't possibly have bones.

Inhaling deeply, the creature began to swing in a slow, wide circle. It swayed in the direction of the wagon and snapped rigid as its entire body stretched itself out like a snake, adding a full pace to its length. The Shadule let out a rattling hiss, then flung its body in the opposite direction so the back of its head nearly touched the ground. It sprang forward, shooting toward the back of the wagon.

As the creature was about to fly through the opening, a burning arrow was loosed from inside and struck it square in the chest. The Shadule exploded into flames, letting out a high-pitched scream as it disappeared into the back of the wagon.

Arthur didn't breathe; he couldn't have moved if his life depended on it. Inside the wagon, the light of the flames flickered brightly, and what he heard made him want to tear at his ears. Wild's agonized screams echoed through the crisp night air. The wagon shook violently as the Shadule shrieked in rage, rattling and snarling.

A moment later, the flames extinguished themselves. It didn't look as if they'd burned out, but rather they'd been sucked inward. As the flames disappeared, Wild's screaming quieted, shifting to a terrified whimper.

"Where is the boy?" the Shadule rasped.

"You're too late," Wild moaned. "The Child of Prophecy has come, and your master's end is near!"

Arthur felt the hair on his body begin to rise as lightning exploded out of the clear night sky, striking near the wagon and forming a crater in the ground. The brightness nearly blinded Arthur, his eyes still sensitive to light. Almost instantly another bolt struck the ground behind him, flinging a mound of dirt high in the air. The very air was alive with electricity, and in the brightness of the lightning strikes, Arthur saw three Oriax slowly approaching.

He ducked low and didn't think the beasts had seen him, but they were coming directly toward him. As he turned back to look at the wagon, he screamed. The Shadule was standing next to the wagon, but staring directly at Arthur and Jack. Taking a fluid step toward him, it dropped to its belly and began slithering forward, moving like a snake.

In blind panic, Arthur leaped from the hole, pulling Jack behind him.

"I will receive great reward for this," the Shadule hissed, its forked tongue flicking out from between its lifeless, gray lips. "Since time before time we have waited!" it rattled.

As it slithered closer, another bolt of lightning fell, booming loudly and landing between Arthur and the Shadule. Though the creature glanced warily at the sky, it barely slowed its approach. More lightning fell, crashing all around them.

The Shadule rose fluidly into a standing position and continued forward, walking the final steps to stand over the boys. With a look of pure ecstasy, it bent low, and without so much as a glance at Arthur, the Shadule scooped Jack into its arms.

Arthur wanted to scream, to call out to Mrs. Dumphry, to do something to help Jack. But how could he stand against evil such as this?

Cradling Jack, the creature began walking away as the black wings unfurled from its body.

Alexia stood on the topmost branch of a birch tree, her sling ready in one hand as she idly thumbed a stone with the other. She'd been standing in the tree for more than an hour and was beginning to wonder if the old woman had tricked her. Maybe she'd just wanted to leave Alexia behind.

As they'd walked into the woods, Alexia had kept as close an eye on the old woman as she had on the surrounding forest. After ten minutes of walking, Mrs. Dumphry had stopped. There was nothing different about this part of the woods that Alexia could see, but the woman seemed to be able to hear, or perhaps sense something. Leaning close, she'd whispered, "The Oriax are hard to kill. But if you hit them squarely between the eyes, they will die quick enough. However, if your stone lands even an inch off center, the beasts will barely feel it." Mrs. Dumphry's eyes searched the forest as she spoke. "They are close now. At least one pack has been hunting us since Ballylesson."

The old woman pointed to a nearby tree and asked Alexia if she thought she might be able to climb it. Alexia sneered and, without waiting for more instructions, she'd quietly taken four running steps and leaped for the closest branch, climbing silently. In a matter of seconds she was standing high in the tree. As she'd climbed, she'd pictured herself looking down to see Mrs. Dumphry staring up in wonder. But when she turned to look, the old woman was nowhere to be seen.

An hour later, Alexia was still standing on her branch and wishing she had stayed to hear more of Mrs. Dumphry's plan before running off. Alexia's anger began to grow. How long must she wait here? Although she didn't trust the woman, she wasn't at all excited about being alone in the woods with those Oriax nearby.

Alexia's anger with Mrs. Dumphry wasn't the only thing on her mind. The old woman had said she could save Megan. That was the only reason Alexia had decided to go with her. And now, here she was hiding in a tree in the middle of the forest! Her confusion and anger fed on one another until she was spitting mad. When she scanned the ground, her breath caught. A large number of Oriax were striding through the forest and would soon pass directly beneath her.

Some of the beasts moved with the fluidity of cats, while others plodded as steady as horses, jumped about like rabbits, or slithered along the ground. Yet whether they looked awkward or stealthy, they barely made a sound. Alexia counted thirty, but she was sure there were more, farther out in the darkness.

She once again wished she hadn't left Mrs. Dumphry so early. Had she stayed, she might have learned how many Oriax were in a pack, or what the old woman expected her to do when they arrived.

As she shifted her footing to get a better view of the beasts below, something pulled at the corner of her vision. When she looked out into the trees, her jaw dropped. She hadn't known the beasts could climb and fly!

At least another twenty Oriax were coming toward her, swinging, jumping, or flitting between the branches. They moved as silently as those on the ground. It was too dark to make out any of them clearly, but all were heading directly toward her. Though they had yet to see her, in a matter of seconds she would be surrounded. The beasts were obviously hunting something. Both the Oriax below and those in the trees stopped every now and then to smell the air before continuing on.

It was too late to move without being seen, but if Alexia stayed still, then what? She squeezed her eyes shut, trying to think. Moving slowly, she stood on her toes and readied herself to spring. Silently slipping a stone into her sling, she let it drop to her side. Had the old hag placed her here so she could be eaten? The thought infuriated her.

Alexia had no more time to think. The first of the beasts had arrived. To her left was an Oriax with the arms and tail of a monkey and the body and head of a tiger. Before it moved to the next branch, another arrived on her right. This Oriax had the wings of an eagle and the body and head of a wolverine. Out of the corner of her eye, she could see even more of them arriving below.

This is the end, she thought.

And then the lightning came. Out of a clear night sky, bright bolts exploded all around her.

Chapter 16

WHERE THERE SHOULD ONLY BE ONE

Arthur watched in absolute terror as the Shadule carried Jack away. All around, lightning exploded, throwing debris high into the air. It was so close he could feel the electricity flowing along his skin.

Not allowing himself to think further, he stood and squeezed his eyes shut. Then, screaming at the top of his lungs, he ran and dove on the Shadule's back. As he slammed into the creature, it stumbled to the ground, and Jack slipped from its arms. Arthur landed on top, with his face pressed against the Shadule's clammy skin.

With a viper's speed, the Shadule melted away and bonelessly whipped around, its mouth open wider than should have been possible as it readied for a deadly attack. Arthur was sure he was about to die when an arrow flew past his head and pierced the creature's shoulder.

A moment later a bolt of lightning struck again. It was so close that both Arthur and the Shadule were flung high into the air before landing in a rainfall of dirt and debris.

Arthur's ears rang loudly as he struggled to his feet.

"Run!" Arthur heard Wild scream.

Wild leaned heavily against the side of the wagon and was bleeding from multiple wounds. His right arm was badly burned, yet he had somehow managed to nock another arrow. Arthur didn't wait to see what happened next. He knew their only hope was to find Mrs. Dumphry. Stumbling into the night, he screamed for help.

Jack opened his eyes groggily. He was lying on his back staring at a lightning-streaked sky. His leg throbbed from a wound he had no memory of receiving. As he rolled onto his side, he saw a strange black-winged creature. It was facing a wild-eyed boy holding a bow and arrow. *I know that boy*, Jack thought. *That's Ethan Wild!*

As Ethan loosed the arrow, the creature moved fluidly to the side, letting it fly past.

"Run!" Ethan yelled at Jack, loosing another arrow.

With fear and adrenaline surging through him, Jack struggled to his feet and ran. And though his leg burned like fire, he made himself keep going. Lightning struck all around, shattering earth and setting trees ablaze.

As Jack ran, a beast that looked to be part monkey and part hawk flew out of the trees above him. When it saw Jack, it screeched loudly, flapped its wings, and sped toward him.

This must be a nightmare, Jack thought as he ran. But nightmare or not, Jack Staples still ran.

The tree shook violently as lightning struck the earth below. Alexia clung to the trunk, somehow managing to stay on her branch. *It's not possible!* The thought pounded through her head. *How can lightning strike when there is no storm?*

The two Oriax that had been on either side of Alexia were gone, each killed by one of the bolts. Yet many more creatures were arriving in the surrounding trees. One of them, part gorilla and part vulture, spotted Alexia, and leaped at her from a nearby branch.

Although fear surged inside her, she also felt bone-deep rage. *The old woman thinks she can kill me this easily? I'll show her!* Clearing her mind of all distractions, Alexia gave herself to the trees. This was her true home. She'd lived in the trees longer than she'd lived anywhere. If these beasts thought they could come into her home and kill her, she would show them just how wrong they were.

As the Oriax swung toward her, Alexia dropped a stone into the fold of her sling and ran down the length of the branch. As she reached the end, she turned and leaped outward, swinging the sling around even as she flew backward through the air. In one fluid motion, she loosed the stone and spun around to grab hold of the branch of a nearby elm.

Although her stone struck the Oriax in the face, she'd missed the center of its vulture head. The beast shrieked, then looped its gorilla arms around the branch and shuffled toward her. It dove at Alexia as she stepped off the branch and dropped. When the Oriax landed, it looked around in confusion, its blood-red eyes searching for the girl who had been there a moment earlier. Alexia was now hanging from the branch by one arm, her hand gripped just between the Oriax's feet.

When the beast looked down, she swung the sling with all her might, and this time her stone struck true. As the Oriax fell from the branch, Alexia crawled back up, then turned and vomited out everything that was in her stomach.

Lightning continued to strike, and all around the forest, entire trees burst into flames. As Alexia searched the surrounding trees, she gasped, almost losing her balance. Mrs. Dumphry was standing in the forest, surrounded by Oriax. At least fifty of the beasts were running, hopping, slithering, and flying at her from every direction.

The old woman spun and leaped about like an acrobat, streams of white-hot flames exploding from her palms and crashing into the beasts. Dead Oriax lay scattered all around, yet for every Oriax that went down, two more came to take its place.

Alexia didn't have time to continue watching—an Oriax with the head of a pig and the body of a squirrel climbed steadily toward her. As she scanned the surrounding trees, she spotted four more of the beasts hunting her. Alexia slipped another stone into her sling and ran through the trees.

Arthur ran blindly, screaming for Mrs. Dumphry, though his screams were lost among the crackling booms of lightning. When he finally saw his teacher, she was surrounded by Oriax.

Arthur watched in wonder as spiderwebs of flame exploded into the beasts. The fire was coming from Mrs. Dumphry! As she spun, for just a moment she spotted Arthur, and when their eyes met, her expression shifted from determination to shock.

The world suddenly flashed a brilliant white, and Arthur had the distinct sensation of flying, just before he slammed into something solid. Lying flat on his back, the sky spun around him as the rain of lightning ceased. Arthur blinked up at the night sky and felt a sticky wet substance dripping from his face. When he touched his left eye, he was surprised to find his hand covered in blood.

"Where is the Staples boy? I told you to stay with him!"

Arthur tried to focus his good eye on Mrs. Dumphry. Her hair was out of its bun and hanging wildly around her shoulders, and her face was streaked in grime. "The creature with the"—he cut off, trying to make his voice work—"with the white eyes. It's got Jack!"

"Where?" A look of horror crossed his teacher's face as she bounded to her feet.

"At the wagon," Arthur croaked. Mrs. Dumphry picked up her skirts and ran.

Jack stumbled through the forest, running as fast as his wounded leg would allow. From high up in the trees, the strange creature that was a mixture of monkey and bird flew toward him.

"You cannot hide from me, child," a voice rasped from behind. "I have known your smell since before Time was born!"

Jack turned to see the milk-eyed creature slithering behind him. His leg screamed at him to stop, but adrenaline and fear pushed him forward. The forest blazed as whole trees burned brightly. Between the flying beast above, the slithering creature behind, and the fire all around, Jack was quickly running out of options.

"You belong with us," the creature called. Jack didn't look back, but he could hear its voice close behind. "You cannot run from your destiny! You are the Child of Prophecy!"

Jack dropped to the ground as the monkey-headed beast swooped down and missed him by a hair. He tried to stand again, but his leg protested and he collapsed. As he struggled to rise, Jack knew it was too late.

A split second before the flying beast arrived again, the milk-eyed creature streaked through the air, knocking the beast aside. "Mine!" it screamed. "The Child of Prophecy is mine!"

Jack struggled to his feet as the creature picked up the flying beast and flung it against a nearby tree.

Rounding on Jack, the creature's great wings unfurled from its body as it glided toward him. In the light of the blazing trees, Jack could see it clearly for the first time. Its skin was pale gray, its ears overly large and pointed, and its head more oval than round. The wings looked as though they were a second layer of skin, and as they grew, the creature turned from pale gray to ghostly white.

Exhausted and in immense pain, Jack stayed pressed to the ground. Whatever this creature wanted, Jack was simply too tired and in too much pain to try to stop it.

"Get away from him!" a voice screamed from somewhere high in the trees.

Jack looked up to see Alexia swing around a branch, her crimson cape billowing behind her. As she landed on a lower branch, she launched herself at the creature. Somersaulting in midair, she sent a stone flying at its head. The creature, moving almost lazily, swatted the stone aside and snatched Alexia out of the air with one arm, slamming her to the ground.

Dazed and winded, Alexia lay on her back, gasping for breath. Keeping its feet rooted, the creature bent its body low so it hovered over her. Its great wings were fully extended; it snarled in rage, opening its mouth wide.

As it was about to attack, the winged creature met Alexia's eyes and suddenly shrieked in fear. All grace vanished as it flung itself away and scrambled to its feet. "No!" it cried, pointing an accusing finger at Alexia. "It can't be! It's not possible!" it rattled as it took another step back.

Alexia struggled to sit up. Jack crawled over, groaning every time he placed weight on his wounded leg. He grabbed Alexia's hand and squeezed tight. She squeezed back.

"Who are you?" the creature snarled.

Still holding on to Jack's hand, Alexia stood, pulling him up to stand beside her. Jack gritted his teeth to keep from passing out from the pain, but managed to stay standing.

"This can't be," the creature moaned as its milky white eyes shifted back and forth between Jack and Alexia.

"Shadule!" a voice roared. "Leave now or die!"

When the creature turned to face Mrs. Dumphry, wariness entered its eyes. Jack's teacher was hunched and very pale, and though her voice had been firm, she looked frail and weary beyond words. As it studied her, the creature grew bolder.

"You!" It took a fluid step toward her. "You thought you could hide her from us," it rasped. "She changes everything! Two children, where the prophecy speaks of only one."

"Enough," Mrs. Dumphry said firmly, calmly. Her voice was the same as when she spoke to an unruly pupil. Yet as she extended both hands toward it, the creature halted its menacing approach.

"You don't have the strength to face me," it rattled.

"You, of all the Assassin's creatures, must know who I am. Or does the worm think itself a bird?" Mrs. Dumphry stood up straight as a hard look entered her eyes. "Come closer, little worm, and see how weary I am." Her voice was mocking. "You are only alive because I have use of you. Go back and tell your master what you saw here. Tell him the Last Battle is near. The scales are coming off, and the Author's army grows stronger every day. The Great Awakening will not be stopped. Tell your master of the second child. Tell him that together, these children will destroy him and all of the Shadow Souled once and for all!"

"We know the prophecies as well as you!" the creature croaked as it turned its milky eyes on Jack and Alexia. "The child will bow before the Assassin and destroy the world! One or two—it changes nothing." The creature's wings began to beat as it rose slowly into the air. "And the child will be the end of the Awakened!" Keeping a wary eye on Mrs. Dumphry, it rose, then disappeared into the night sky.

Everyone's eyes stayed glued to the sky. Mrs. Dumphry stood perfectly still, scanning the heavens. Arthur had also arrived and was now standing beside Mrs. Dumphry, squinting upward with his one good eye. After a moment Mrs. Dumphry began to sway, and with her eyes still on the sky, she nodded, then looked at Jack and Alexia. "We are safe now. The Shadule is gone." When she finished speaking, she collapsed to the ground, unconscious.

Chapter 17

THE WAR OF TIME

When Mrs. Dumphry collapsed, none of the children moved. All three stared at her, not knowing what to do. After a moment, Jack turned to look in the opposite direction.

"Something's coming," he whispered, trying to stand up straighter. Alexia gritted her teeth as Arthur stumbled over to stand next to them. He'd found a large stick and was gripping it tightly. All three children stood shoulder to shoulder, Alexia in the middle. Whatever was making the sound was coming from the direction of the wagon.

Keeping his eyes glued to the forest in front of him, Jack spoke softly, "Thanks for trying to save me."

"You're welcome," both Alexia and Arthur said at the same time. They shared a look as Alexia nodded to Arthur, who immediately blushed and looked away.

All three were the worse for wear. The wound on Jack's leg had broken open, and Alexia was covered in scrapes and bruises. The left side of Arthur's face was so bruised and swollen that his eye was completely shut. Besides this, all three were covered in dirt and mud. Bending stiffly, Jack picked up a large rock lying at his feet.

Whatever was coming was close now. Alexia stepped forward and began swinging her sling. Jack tensed as a large branch was pushed aside. In the light of the burning trees, Ethan Wild appeared, limping slowly toward them. His chest and neck were badly burned, and a long gash went from his left shoulder all the way down to the elbow of his right arm. He had to use his staff to keep upright. As his eyes landed on the group, he stopped and leaned heavily against a tree.

"I thought you'd all been taken or were dead by now." He let out a long breath. "Where's Mrs. ..." His eyes darted to Mrs. Dumphry, lying unconscious on the ground. He stumbled over, almost falling in the process. "Tell me what happened," he demanded, placing a hand on her forehead. Mrs. Dumphry had no obvious wounds, but she did look quite pale.

"You're Ethan Wild," Jack said slowly. "You're the boy who went mad! I thought you were in an asylum somewhere."

He glanced at Jack irritably. "I go by Wild now, but you haven't answered my question."

Alexia's sling continued to spin, and the fierceness hadn't left her eyes. "Where were you? The beasts attack, and you only show up now?" she snarled.

Wild stood tiredly. "Put the sling down, girl."

Alexia whipped her sling around, sending a stone smashing into Wild's thigh.

"Ow!" he yelped. "What was that for?"

"You're lucky I didn't aim for your head." Alexia's tone was menacing. "Answer the question!"

Wild shot her an angry look as he rubbed the bruise already forming on his thigh. "What does it look like I was doing? I was trying to stop the Shadule," he said angrily. "Just ask them," he said, pointing to Jack and Arthur. "If I hadn't been there, these two would be dead! As it is, the thing nearly killed me." He motioned toward his wounds.

Both Jack and Arthur nodded, but Alexia barely acknowledged them as she let loose another stone, this one flying toward Wild's stomach. He was ready this time, swinging his staff around to deflect it. Wild didn't stop his whirling staff but sped it up until it became a blur. Even using only one arm, he was quite good.

Arthur took a step back, and Jack sat down, the pain in his leg too much to continue standing.

"Listen to me." Wild tried to control his voice. "You are going to have to trust me. If you don't, the Dark Servants will find you and it will be too late. We need to carry Mrs. Dumphry to the wagon and get out of here. She will be fine in a few hours, but she needs rest."

"I killed six of the Oriax, and the creature is gone," Alexia retorted, "and don't think you're safe either. Unless you want to get hurt even more, you're going to answer our questions." Alexia glanced at Jack who quickly nodded in agreement.

"You killed *six* of them?" Wild said incredulously.

"That's right. And if you think your staff will save you, think again."

"We don't have time for this," Wild responded, growing more and more impatient. "We need to get out of here before they come back."

"Then you had better start talking! The Shadule"—Alexia struggled with the name—"said something about prophesies, and it seemed to be scared when it saw me."

Wild almost dropped his staff. "You talked to it?"

Alexia took advantage of Wild's shock and let loose another stone, striking him hard in the hand. Wild screamed, dropping his staff. "Will you stop doing that?" he shouted.

Alexia had another stone in the sling before he could so much as look at the staff. A crazy look entered her eyes as she swung it. "Tell us what's going on! Why do they want us? What prophesies?"

"And my mother"—Jack was surprised at the anger he felt—"what's happened to her?"

"And mine? And the town?" Arthur said boldly, stepping closer to Jack.

Wild cast an anxious glance at Mrs. Dumphry, who was still unconscious.

"Boy," Alexia said, her voice menacing. "The next one will land between your eyes. Now talk!"

Wild sighed. "All right," he said, throwing his good arm in the air. "I'll tell you what I can. But some of it won't make sense until we get to Agartha."

"Okay, then," Alexia said. "Start talking."

"Ballylesson was attacked by the Shadow Souled, those who serve a creature we call the Assassin. At least one Shadule and a number of Oriax were part of the attack. I don't know how many of the townsfolk survived—maybe all of them did. The Dark Servants didn't seem to care about anything other than finding you." He spoke to Jack. "They had no reason to stay after you were gone."

A pained look entered Wild's eyes as he continued. "My uncle was there too, but the only thing we could do for him and everyone else was to leave."

Jack waited for more, but Wild stayed silent.

"And my mother?" Jack asked. "Is she dead?"

When Wild met his eyes, he hesitated. "Yes … At least, I think so."

Jack suddenly felt dizzy.

"She"—Alexia pointed angrily at Mrs. Dumphry—"told me we could save Megan. She said if I came with her, Megan Staples would be saved!"

"She had to tell you something to get you to listen," replied Wild. "If you hadn't come, you'd be dead or captured by now."

Alexia took a menacing step forward, swinging her sling a little faster. "Tell us what's happening. And if you lie to me, it'll be the last thing you do!"

Wild gave one last, longing look at his staff before answering. "The world that most people live in is not real. Or rather, it is only a shadow of the real world. The story goes that before our world was born, something terrible happened. And because of it, at the birth of our world, scales were placed on the eyes of every human and beast. The scales were meant to stop us from seeing the world as it truly is. Except that for some, the scales have fallen off."

"What are you talking about?" Alexia was beyond angry. "You had better start making sense or I'll—"

"You asked for answers," Wild cut her off. "You may not understand them all—to be honest, there are few who do. I don't even know if the Sephari understand all of it, but I'm telling the truth. Now, be quiet and listen."

Alexia stuck out her lower lip but remained silent.

"A war has been raging since before Time was born—a war between light and darkness, between the Author and the Assassin. But when our world was born, the war was brought here, and here it has stayed. I guess you had to find out sooner or later. But you"— now he spoke directly to Alexia—"have changed everything. Jack was expected. The Awakened have been searching for him since the very first humans awakened."

Alexia and Jack shared a confused look.

"There is a prophecy that speaks of a child who will be born without scales. Its eyes will be open from the first day. There are many parts of the prophecy we simply don't understand, and"— Wild shrugged irritably—"I haven't been told everything. But the prophecy says two things that seem to be clear: the child will bow before the Assassin and destroy the world, and the child will destroy the Assassin and save the world.

"Jack was born without scales," he continued. "He is the Child of Prophecy. His mother was the Chosen One. It all made sense. And then, as Mrs. Dumphry tells it"—Wild shifted his gaze back to Alexia—"you showed up in Ballylesson. And your eyes are proof; you were also born without scales."

Jack listened in confused silence.

"Until now the prophecy never made sense," Wild told them. "How could the child both destroy and save the world? But now there are two children where there should only be one. Does this mean one of you will join us and the other will fight against us? Or does it mean something else?"

Jack and Alexia shared a disbelieving look, and Arthur took an involuntary step back.

"There's not much more I know. My scales only fell off a few years ago, and I haven't been told everything." Wild seemed irritated at this. "When she awakens, Mrs. Dumphry will tell you more, but we need to leave now. We've stayed too long already."

"You say my eyes are proof," Alexia snapped. "But my eyes aren't any different than yours."

"And how often have you looked at your eyes?" Wild retorted. "You can tell if someone has awakened by the scars they bear. When we're safely away from here, I'll happily show you my scars. They're on the center of my eyes and very faint, but they are there. It's the same with every Awakened. But the two of you don't have scars. It's not something I'd be able to see from here, but if I looked closely, I would see a faint colored streak crossing your pupils."

"Everyone's eyes are like that," Alexia retorted, though she sounded less sure than before.

Wild rolled his eyes irritably. "No, everyone's eyes are not like that. In all the world, only you and Jack have eyes like that." As he spoke, he picked up Mrs. Dumphry and threw her over his good shoulder. "These questions could go on for days, and you still wouldn't be satisfied. I'm done for the night. We're leaving."

As Jack followed Wild back to the wagon, he felt sick to his stomach. He remembered his mother's words from the night before she died. "You are not a normal boy, Jack. Your birth was prophesied even before our world came into being." Besides this, Jack had seen the colored smear at the center of his eyes. It was faint and could only be seen in full daylight, but there was a small, aqua-blue streak crossing the pupil of each eye. He'd never thought anything of it until this moment.

A few hours later, Mrs. Dumphry and all three children were asleep in the back of the wagon as Wild drove. Wild had found some pine branches and made a bed for Mrs. Dumphry on the floorboards. Jack and Arthur shared one bench, and Alexia took the other.

When he climbed in, Jack was sure he would never be able to find sleep. His mother was dead; he was in the middle of some kind of waking nightmare, and his leg still burned like fire. Yet as his mind spun with thoughts of home, he closed his eyes and immediately fell into a fitful sleep.

When he opened his eyes again, Jack was surprised to see that the sun was up. Every muscle in his body ached. Arthur slept with his head resting on Jack's legs; Alexia now lay on the floor on top of the pine branches; Mrs. Dumphry was no longer there; and the wagon wasn't moving. Jack's chest tightened as a tear slid down his cheek. All he could think about was the sight of his mother lying on the grass outside his house.

Every muscle protested as he sat up. He was ravenously hungry. When he moved his legs out from under Arthur's head, Jack let out a quiet moan. Although the burning in his leg didn't seem quite as bad as the night before, the wound had turned very dark.

When Arthur's head hit the bench, he mumbled something but didn't wake. Jack rubbed his good leg, trying to get the blood flowing. From outside, he could hear a low murmur of conversation. He cautiously put weight on the wounded leg. Although it burned, the pain was bearable at least. Creeping quietly so as not to wake the others, he stepped from the wagon and stretched his arms above his head, groaning at the stiffness in his muscles.

Whoever was speaking was hidden inside a small copse of trees a short distance away. Jack walked toward the trees as quietly as he could. He wanted to hear what was being said without being seen. As he peered from behind a tree, he saw Mrs. Dumphry speaking with a man he'd never seen before. The man was tall with shoulder-length black hair, olive skin, and a large scar running from his forehead over a ruined eye and down his cheek. He was dressed completely in black, with a long cape and a sword buckled at his waist.

Wild stood nearby, keeping watch. Each time his back was turned, Jack crept slowly closer.

"You should have told us!" The man sounded angry.

"And what would you have done?" Mrs. Dumphry asked. "Sent an army to collect them? You would have drawn the attention of the Assassin himself. This was the only way."

"I'd have sent more than a single boy." The dark-haired man glanced at Wild, who was pretending not to listen. "You stubborn woman, I'd have come myself if I had known."

"I trust Wild with my life," Mrs. Dumphry replied. "And right or wrong, it's done. I'd hoped to leave undetected, but I was too late.

The Dark Servants were quicker than I had imagined. It shouldn't have been possible for them to beat me back to Ballylesson, but by the time I arrived, they were already there."

The man was still angry, but his tone shifted as he put his hand on Mrs. Dumphry's cheek. "If I'd lost you, I would be lost. And you aren't just important to me, but to all of us."

Jack watched as Mrs. Dumphry leaned against the man and placed her head against his chest. "And yet, compared to these two children, I am nothing," she whispered. Jack was confused. Mrs. Dumphry must be three or even four times older than this man, yet it looked to him as if they loved each other.

"Two," the man said with a hint of awe in his voice. "How did we not see it? And how did the girl stay hidden for so long?"

"I do not know." Mrs. Dumphry shook her head. "There is more happening here than we could possibly understand. Yet I am sure Alexia and Jack are both the Child of Prophecy."

As Jack tried to move closer, a twig snapped beneath his wounded leg. Wild stepped forward and hefted his staff, and the man placed a hand on his sword.

"You can come out now," Mrs. Dumphry called, her voice stone cold.

Jack sighed and straightened from his crouch, stepping from behind the tree. He did his best to meet his teacher's eyes.

The man shot an irritable glance at Wild. "You trust this boy with your life, yet he can't keep you safe from a skulking child."

Mrs. Dumphry tsked as she looked at Jack. "Go to the wagon and wake the others," she said cooly. "We are leaving."

Chapter 18

WALLYDROM

Jack returned to the wagon to find Alexia already up. She was rummaging through one of the saddlebags, looking for something to eat. As she pulled out a large chunk of cheese, Jack's stomach growled loudly. He was famished. The night before when he'd crawled into the wagon, he'd been hungry enough to eat a horse. In this moment he thought he might be able to eat two.

Alexia turned and looked at him, her face unreadable. After a moment she broke off a chunk of cheese and handed it to him. Jack nodded his thanks, taking a large bite. Although his leg still burned, he was beginning to wonder if it might be getting better. It looked as bad as before—worse maybe—but he could put a little weight on it now.

Hobbling over to the wagon, he grabbed Arthur's leg and shook him slightly. "Arthur, you need to wake up."

"Don't eat me!" Arthur screamed as he sat bolt upright. When he saw Jack, he glared at him with his good eye. "That's not funny!"

"I wasn't trying to scare you," Jack said. "Mrs. Dumphry wants us to get ready. She says we're leaving soon."

"I'm not going anywhere until that old hag gives me answers," Alexia said. "If she thinks she can lie to me, she's sorely mistaken."

"And when did I lie to you, child?" Mrs. Dumphry came striding through the trees behind Alexia with the stranger and Wild on either side.

Alexia turned and slipped a stone into the fold of her sling. "You told me Megan Staples could be saved! You said if I came with you, you'd help her." Swinging her sling, Alexia took a threatening step forward.

Mrs. Dumphry stopped walking, and the stranger and Wild both stepped away, watching with a look of interest. "No, child, I am afraid you misheard. I told you if you wanted to help Megan Staples, you would come with me. There was never any chance of saving her life. Her light was fading even before I arrived." Mrs. Dumphry sounded as if she were giving a lecture in the schoolhouse. "When I found you, the only way to help Megan was to keep the two of you alive. It is all she would have wanted. So you see, I did not lie; you merely heard what you wanted to."

Jack's chest tightened with every word. How could she speak so coldly? How could she say these terrible things? "What's wrong with you?" he asked angrily. "I thought you were her friend!"

Mrs. Dumphry grimaced slightly, shifting her gaze to Jack. "I am sorry, Jack. I needn't have spoken so bluntly. I am beyond weary, and I was harsher than I should have been. Your mother was one of the truest friends I have ever had. Regardless, what I said is true. Your mother is gone. If I could have saved her, I would have. I don't know what happened or how she died, but I have no doubt she gave her life to save the two of you. But we haven't the luxury of time to properly grieve. We must mourn even as we flee."

"No!" Jack erupted with an anger he didn't know was there. "No. I don't believe you. We have to go back! Maybe she's still alive. We can try … something! And what about my father and Parker and the rest of them? We have to go back."

Arthur crawled stiffly out of the back of the wagon. "Jack's right," he said. "We have to go back to Ballylesson."

"I don't know about your father or brother or anyone else in Ballylesson," said Mrs. Dumphry. "But going back will only hurt those you love, and it will surely kill you. The Dark Servants came for you." Her eyes stayed on Jack. "And now that they know you exist too," she said to Alexia, "they won't stop until they have you both."

Without warning, Alexia screamed and sent the small stone flying at Mrs. Dumphry's head. Just as the stone was about to strike her, it stopped in midair. Arthur let out a small gasp of surprise, and Jack stepped back. Alexia merely looked angry.

"Child"—Mrs. Dumphry's voice was even colder than before— "I understand that Wild told you some things he should not have. And now you must have more questions than ever. Once we are on our way, I will answer many of them, but right now we are leaving.

The Dark Servants have not been beaten, only beaten back. Even now they draw near."

Mrs. Dumphry turned and motioned to the stranger. "This is Aias. He is a friend and was kind enough to bring horses. From here we ride."

As Mrs. Dumphry climbed on to a white mare, the stone Alexia had flung at Mrs. Dumphry dropped to the ground.

An hour later, the wagon had been left behind, and all six travelers rode horseback through the forest. Jack rode a dark-brown stallion with a white spot just above its left eye. He had never been a good rider, and because he could only put a little weight on his wounded leg, he was even worse than usual. But the horse seemed to sense his injury. The only reason he was able to stay in his saddle was because the stallion moved far more gracefully than any horse Jack had ridden.

Arthur rode a dun-colored packhorse in front of Jack. He was an even worse rider and bounced continuously, nearly falling off with every other step. Alexia, on the other hand, looked as if she had ridden every day of her life. Her back was straight, and she didn't bounce at all. She rode a dappled gray gelding at least two hands shorter than Jack's stallion. Mrs. Dumphry and Aias led the way, and Wild brought up the rear.

Not long after they'd left the wagon, Mrs. Dumphry called back: "Children." Her voice was harsh in the silence of the fields where they rode, causing Alexia, Arthur, and Jack to jump. "I told you I would answer your questions when we were on our way. And now we are on our way."

All three children booted their horses forward. They were riding through a large field of potatoes. In the distance Jack could see a farmer's house with smoke rising from the chimney. Until this moment he hadn't thought about where they were; he'd only been thinking about what was happening. They had been traveling for two days and a night, though, and he was curious.

"Where are we?" He was almost afraid to hear the answer.

"We are drawing near the town of Wallydrom."

Jack felt even more alone than he had just moments earlier. Until now he'd never been more than a few hours outside Ballylesson. The day his mother took him to the circus had been a grand adventure. In part because they were going to a real circus and in part because it was the farthest away from home he had ever been.

"What's going on?" Alexia demanded, interrupting Jack's thoughts. "What were those beasts, and how did you stop that stone? And the fire and lightning and all of it! You have to tell us what's happening!"

"I suppose I do. Yet you will need to be patient. Pull one thread and a hundred unravel." After a moment Mrs. Dumphry smiled. "But I suppose even the grandest tapestry began with a single thread."

Alexia glared at her.

"Both of you"—her gaze took in Jack and Alexia—"are different. The rest of the world is born into darkness, blind as babes. Yet when the two of you were born, there were no scales covering your eyes. You have lived in the true world from the very first day."

"I've never seen scales on anyone's eyes," Alexia said haughtily.

"They are not scales you can see—at least not until they have fallen off—but they blind nonetheless. Young Mr. Greaves understands this more than anyone, I would think. The scales covering his eyes have only recently fallen off. And though he is still relearning how to see, the entire world is already feeling more ... substantial. Arthur is now one of the Awakened. In a way, you could say he has been reborn. And as with every newborn, he must learn how to walk and talk in this bright new world."

Arthur turned a strange color of green as he listened to Mrs. Dumphry's words.

"It's not that there are two worlds, though this is often how it has been explained in the past. Rather, Arthur was only living in a shadow of the real word, whereas now, he is living in all of it."

Mrs. Dumphry paused for a moment, then looked at Arthur. "Young Mr. Greaves, you did well last night. It would seem Wild was right. It is a good thing that you have joined us."

Arthur blushed as Mrs. Dumphry turned back to Jack and Alexia. "However, Mr. Greaves is not like the two of you. For you, the world has always been one. Your eyes have always seen the world as it truly is."

"That doesn't make sense," Jack protested. "I don't see things differently from other people."

"And how would you know if you did?" Mrs. Dumphry replied.

Jack opened his mouth to protest but didn't know what to say. Of course he would know ... wouldn't he?

"When you and Alexia first saw the Oriax and the Shadule, you saw beasts and creatures of pure evil. But if an Oriax were to pass in front of someone whose eyes are blinded by scales, that person would see a mangy-looking dog. And if a Shadule had stood in front of Arthur before his scales had fallen off, he would have seen a gaunt and sickly looking man dressed in rags."

Arthur nodded when he met Jack's eyes. Whatever he'd seen, Arthur seemed certain that Mrs. Dumphry was telling the truth.

"On the day you were born, young Jack," Mrs. Dumphry continued, "the Assassin himself came out of hiding to find you. Many of the Awakened died trying to keep you safe. And with their help, your mother and I escaped and found a place to hide you from the world. After all, you are the Child of Prophecy."

"And what about me?" Alexia asked bitterly. "If I'm supposedly a part of this stupid prophecy, how come I had no one to protect me?"

Mrs. Dumphry sighed. "To be honest, I don't know. When Jack was hidden in Ballylesson, Blinding Stones were placed around the town. Blinding Stones are used to blind the eyes of evil. In your case, Alexia, you had no such stones that I know of. Not only do I not understand how you exist, but you are older than Jack. By your eyes it is clear you are also the Child of Prophecy, yet somehow you have managed to stay hidden and alive for all these years."

Jack's mind was spinning. Every word from Mrs. Dumphry brought a hundred new questions. What was a Blinding Stone? What did the prophecy say, and who gave it? Who was the Assassin, and who died trying to keep him safe?

"The prophecy is in a language not of our world, and few here understand it," Mrs. Dumphry continued. "In essence it says a child will be born without scales, and the child shall save the world and defeat the Assassin, and the child shall bow before the Assassin and destroy the world."

"That doesn't make sense," Alexia said.

"Prophecies rarely do. Yet when young Jack was born, we were certain he was the child the Awakened had been waiting for—for thousands of years. And as I said, on the day he was born, we hid him away." Mrs. Dumphry's face was unreadable as she looked at Alexia. "And then you came along. The fact that you exist, girl, that you showed up in the same town as young Jack just before the Dark Servants arrived, is either the biggest coincidence the world has ever known, or something much grander is happening here. And I have always believed *coincidence* is the word we use when we are too blind to see the full story."

Mrs. Dumphry's voice was tight as she continued. "Your existence changes everything."

"None of this matters!" Jack blurted. "I don't care about any of your stupid prophecies or war. My mother is dead, and you took me away from her. All of Ballylesson could be dying! Don't you care?"

Mrs. Dumphry's eyes hardened. "I care more than you could possibly know. Ballylesson has been my home for many, many years. But caring is not enough." Mrs. Dumphry's knuckles whitened on her horse's reins. She was angrier than Jack had ever seen her. "But I will not allow you to run off and get yourself killed trying to—" She stopped, turning to look to the horizon. A moment later, Aias came galloping toward them.

"Wait here," Mrs. Dumphry commanded as she nudged her horse forward to meet him.

When Mrs. Dumphry was safely out of earshot, Alexia whispered, "We need to leave." Her voice was quiet but full of resolve. "I don't believe a word she says. All of this is happening because of her."

"I don't think so." Jack felt his throat tighten. "On the night before my mother died, she told me that I was special. She mentioned a prophecy and said I could do things that no one else can. She said there were things I was born to do. And then she mentioned you, Alexia."

"And what did she say?" Alexia's eyes narrowed to slits.

"She said you were special as well, and she wanted to tell us everything in the morning …" Jack wiped a tear from his cheek.

"How could she have known anything about me?" Alexia asked. "I barely knew her more than a week."

"I don't know," Jack replied. "But she seemed sure you were a part of it all. But I don't care about a stupid prophecy or a war. I don't want to be a part of the Awakened or whatever. I just want to go home!"

Before anyone could say another word, Mrs. Dumphry was back. "Follow me and stay close," she commanded.

A short while later, they were riding down a large dirt road leading into Wallydrom. Arthur had heard his father speak of Wallydrom. He'd said the town was even bigger than Ballylesson and the schoolhouse more than three times the size. Even though he loved and trusted his father, Arthur still hadn't been sure he believed it.

Yet Arthur would never be able to see Wallydrom as his father had. As they rode closer, it became clear that the town had been destroyed. Every house and building had been burned to the ground, and bodies littered the streets. At first Arthur was horrified, thinking the bodies were people, yet he soon realized most were far too large to be human.

The streets of Wallydrom were littered with the bodies of horses, cows, goats, and pigs. All were dead, and many had turned as black as coal. Also lying dead were a large number of Oriax, each with multiple arrows sprouting from between their eyes.

As Mrs. Dumphry spoke, she didn't look back or slow her horse. "Wallydrom was attacked by the same Shadule and Oriax that came to Ballylesson."

"Where are all the people?" Jack voiced the question Arthur had been thinking.

"I can only hope most of the townsfolk escaped into the woods, though it is obvious some were foolish enough to stay and fight."

"How can you say that?" Alexia said accusingly. "How can you be so cold?"

"I call it foolish because it was, child. If they had not fought back, Wallydrom would still be standing." Mrs. Dumphry was angry again. "The Shadow Souled were looking for the Child of Prophecy. I am certain they were instructed not to kill anyone, but rather to round up the townsfolk. They wouldn't have wanted to risk killing the child by mistake. Yes, the animals might have suffered, and a building or two would have been destroyed, but once the Dark Servants learned Jack wasn't here, they would have quickly moved on.

"Just over a week ago, when I left Ballylesson, one of the things I did was warn the Mayor of Wallydrom of an impending attack," Mrs. Dumphry continued. "Wallydrom has long been a stronghold of the Awakened, and they knew the danger, but still they chose to stay and fight. I suppose they thought they were being brave. And though the line between foolishness and bravery is razor thin, in this case it was pure foolishness."

Mrs. Dumphry reined in her horse and turned to face the others. "I would have ridden around Wallydrom to spare you this gruesome sight, but I need you to see what will happen if you go back to Ballylesson. The Assassin wants you both." Her gaze took in Jack and Alexia. "And he will destroy anyone who tries to stop him. It won't just be the animals they kill, but everyone you know and love."

"How did he find us?" Jack sounded numb. "You said he's been searching for me since I was born. How did he find me now? And why did he think I would be here?"

"We've been here too long already." Aias's voice was grim. "We need to get moving."

Mrs. Dumphry nodded, then answered Jack in a thoughtful voice. "The Assassin has been hunting you since our world was born. His Dark Servants have scoured the earth. But I don't think the Shadowfog came to Ballylesson randomly. I think something happened on the night of the circus fire." Mrs. Dumphry's birdlike eyes were piercing as she looked at Jack. "Somehow, the Assassin knew you were in Ireland. Had I known, I would have taken you away, but I did not. I would guess the Shadow Souled have been hunting throughout Ireland ever since that night."

"On the night I left," Mrs. Dumphry continued, speaking directly to Jack, "when you told me about seeing the Shadowfog in the woods, I went to your house and took some of your clothes. The Shadowfog hunts by smell, and though it is a deadly killer, it is not cunning. The fog pursued me for three full days before it learned it was not chasing you. I'd hoped it wouldn't be able to find its way back to Ballylesson. I'd hoped to buy more time. But I was sorely mistaken. Somehow, the Dark Servants arrived in Ballylesson even before I did."

Mrs. Dumphry nodded to Aias. "We must ride hard for the next few hours. With luck, we will reach the underground city of Agartha before nightfall."

Chapter 19

A LONG WAY DOWN

No one said a word for the next three hours. The only sound was the steady plodding of the horses' hooves. Aias had disappeared, scouting the way ahead, while Wild hung far at the back, keeping watch behind. Mrs. Dumphry led the way, followed closely by the three children.

An hour after they left Wallydrom, they'd galloped into a field of towering maize. They had been in the same field for more than three hours already, and for the entire ride, Mrs. Dumphry's words had been tumbling through Alexia's head.

"The fact that you exist, girl, that you showed up in the same town as young Jack just before the Dark Servants arrived is either the biggest coincidence the world has ever known, or there is something much grander happening."

The woman is insane, she thought for what must have been the hundredth time. Alexia had simply been chasing her friend Killer, trying to keep him safe. Nothing had led her to Ballylesson. The more she thought about it, the more she didn't understand, and the more she didn't understand, the angrier she became. Glaring at Mrs. Dumphry's back, she booted her horse forward just as Mrs. Dumphry slowed. Alexia barely managed to pull her reins in time to avoid colliding with the woman and her horse.

"Are you trying to kill me?" Alexia seethed. Though she knew it had been her fault, she was much too embarrassed about almost losing control of her horse not to blame someone else.

"A mindless tongue and a sleeping bear have nothing in common," Mrs. Dumphry said. "Yet if the tongue does not mind where it wags, it may awaken the bear."

Alexia hated the way the old woman spoke in riddles. "You never answered my questions," she snarled, "about the fire and the lightning. You never told me how you stopped the rock."

Mrs. Dumphry smiled wryly. "Mind the bear, child. I will answer your questions when you ask politely."

"I am hardly a child." Alexia's lower lip protruded slightly. "I am thirteen years old!"

"My dear girl"—Mrs. Dumphry sounded shocked—"age makes an adult in much the same way a glass of water makes an ocean. It is your temper that keeps you locked inside your glass."

Who did this woman think she was? Alexia could hold her temper if she wanted. She just didn't want to, that's all. She waited, but

Mrs. Dumphry merely stared forward and continued her steady plod through the tall stalks of maize.

Alexia wanted to scream at the old hag, but she knew if she did, there would be no answers. Doing her best to swallow her rage, she tempered her voice. "Please, would you tell me how you did the fire, the lightning, and the rock?" Although she had been trying to sound meek, she merely ended up sounding like a strangled cat.

"I suppose that will do," Mrs. Dumphry chortled. "You see, I, too, was once asleep to the real world. It was more years ago than you could imagine and a far less civilized time than we have now." Mrs. Dumphry grimaced at the memory. "And I was a far less cheerful person than I am today."

Alexia wondered if she was trying to make a joke.

"Just before I awakened, I did something terrible, an act of the purest evil." The sun slipped behind the clouds at Mrs. Dumphry's words.

"What did you do?" Alexia asked.

"What did I do?" Mrs. Dumphry smiled sadly. "I will tell you someday. But now is not the time for such a sad story. Not long after my terrible act, the scales fell from my eyes. And just before the blindness came, I saw something … it was the most beautiful …" Mrs. Dumphry grinned, lost in the memory. After a moment she snorted. "My eyes felt like they were on fire, and I was heartbroken at what I had done. And though I had awakened, I had no one to teach me what that meant. As the years passed, I began to discover there were things I could see and do that others could not."

"You mean like the fire and lightning?" Alexia could see Mrs. Dumphry in her mind's eye. Oriax surrounded the old woman as she spun, hurling sprays of fire as lightning exploded throughout the forest.

"Like the fire," Mrs. Dumphry agreed, "but not the lightning. The lightning you saw was not mine."

Alexia waited for more, but Mrs. Dumphry remained silent. "What do you mean it wasn't yours? It was all around you."

"Child, you should understand by now that the eyes can deceive as easily as the tongue. I had nothing to do with the lightning—but that is not my secret to tell."

Alexia bit her tongue to keep from sticking it out at the old woman. She hated being referred to as a child! Yet she needed to know everything if she was going to be able to escape.

"But how do you do it? How did you throw the fire and stop the stone?" She wanted to know this most of all. If she could learn how Mrs. Dumphry did these things, perhaps she could learn how to stop her.

"How does a fish breathe underwater? How does a bird fly? It is a part of me, an imprint on my soul. But this is something you already know. You have been using some of your gifts—Soulprints, we call them—since the day you were born."

Alexia glared at her. "What are you talking about? I don't do anything."

"My dear girl, you can't possibly think your agility is normal. Have you met anyone who has your balance or can climb like you?"

Alexia didn't know what to say. She had always been a good climber. Since before she could remember, she'd climbed everything she could find. That's why her father had called her Ally Goat. It wasn't anything "special"; she was just good at it, that's all.

"I don't believe you. You are trying to trick me," Alexia said scornfully.

Mrs. Dumphry smiled. "Climbing is just the tiniest part of the Soulprints that lie hidden inside you. Soon," she said, "you will begin your training and will awaken to many more."

"You're lying." Alexia was growing angrier by the second, and it was becoming almost impossible to hold her temper.

"You probably have climbed since before you can remember. Yet you fully awakened to your Soulprint when you experienced an intense emotion. It might have been joy, sorrow, or pain. At first you couldn't control it. Sometimes it happened on its own, or maybe while you were sleeping or angry. In your case, I would guess you woke up in some very strange and high places."

Alexia tried to keep her expression neutral. She would not give this woman the satisfaction of thinking she was right. Yes, she had woken up in the treetops on many occasions, but that was not because she was different. It just happened, that's all.

Without warning, Mrs. Dumphry pulled her reins and dismounted. Alexia quickly did the same, and a moment later, Jack, Arthur, and Wild arrived. Aias had been riding ahead and was nowhere to be seen.

"We have arrived at the entrance to the city of Agartha," Mrs. Dumphry announced. "This city has been an Oasis of the Awakened for thousands of years. Children, you will be glad to know that our journey is almost at an end."

When Jack climbed off his horse, he was surprised to find his leg was not hurting at all. In fact, as he'd ridden, he'd barely thought about it. His mind was on much more pressing issues. Though the leg was badly swollen and the veins around the bite were beginning to pop out, when he took a few cautious steps, he barely felt a twinge.

When Mrs. Dumphry saw him looking at his leg in wonder, she quickly walked over and knelt beside him. The moment her fingers touched the blackened flesh, she hissed.

"We haven't much time."

"It doesn't hurt at all," Jack assured her. "I think it's almost better."

"The poison of the Oriax is deceptive. The better you feel, the closer you are to death. The evil in your leg is starting to spread." There was urgency in her voice. "Soon, you will be in more pain than you have ever felt before. It will happen quickly, and if left unchecked, your leg will burst into flames. But this is the last part of our journey. When we reach the bottom, you will be healed. You must remember this, no matter what happens! All you must do is make it to the bottom."

Jack was confused. His leg felt perfectly fine. Perhaps his teacher was mistaken. Besides, they were in the middle of a maize field, not on a mountain. What was he meant to climb down?

Just then, Aias arrived and leaped from his horse. As he walked toward Mrs. Dumphry, he reminded Jack of a wolf.

"They're close. I estimate they'll be here within the hour." Aias ignored everyone, giving all of his attention to Mrs. Dumphry. "I counted four Shadule, two Drogule, and at least ten packs of Oriax. And unless I miss my guess, there is an Odius with them."

Arthur paled, trying to look everywhere at once as Alexia silently mouthed the words, *four Shadule*. Yet Mrs. Dumphry simply nodded. "With any luck, they will lose our trail here."

Jack wiped fresh sweat from his brow.

"What is a Drogule?" Arthur asked. "And a Odi ...," he said, trailing off.

Mrs. Dumphry ignored Arthur as she reached out and grabbed an ear of maize. It was one of many on a stalk that looked no different than any of the tens of thousands of stalks surrounding them; yet, when she pulled it, a small trap door opened soundlessly on the ground in front of her.

The door opened to darkness. Although Jack could see a thin, wooden ladder leading downward, he couldn't tell how deep the pit was. Without a word Aias began climbing down.

Mrs. Dumphry nodded to Jack. "You should go next. And remember, you will find healing at the bottom."

For a moment Jack just looked at her. Sweat stung his eyes, yet his leg still felt fine. As he walked to the trapdoor, he felt a small twinge of pain, though it was hardly worth mentioning. When he looked into the pit, he was surprised to find he could no longer see Aias. Inside it was completely dark. As he placed his foot on the first rung, pain shot through him, and his whole body shuddered. Jack squeezed his eyes shut, letting out a shaky breath. When he opened them again, Mrs. Dumphry was kneeling on the ground in front of him.

"You can do this, Jack Staples! You are stronger than you ever imagined."

Sweat beaded on Jack's forehead as he took a deep breath, nodded to his teacher, and continued down the ladder. With each step, the pain increased. It wasn't a constant pain; rather it shot through his body with every step. Each time it bulleted though him, Jack's hands gripped convulsively around the wooden ladder. Looking upward, he was surprised to see a small hole of light far above. He had made it quite far already. Surely it couldn't be much farther!

As he descended, there was only one thought running through his mind: *I will be healed at the bottom.* He was dripping sweat, and his hands slipped on the wooden rungs as pain wracked his body. With each jolt he shuddered and gripped the ladder so tight he thought his hands might not be able to unclasp themselves. And though he couldn't see it, the wound on his leg had broken open. He could feel a steady trickle of blood dripping into his shoe.

At one point, Jack slipped on a rung and tried to reach out and grab the back wall. He was very concerned to find there was no wall to be found in any direction. His leg screamed at him to stop, and though he couldn't see flames, he felt as if it were burning to a crisp.

Three hours later, Jack was still descending. His body had run out of sweat and his shoe had so completely filled with blood that it made a sloshing sound with each step. He was desperately thirsty and much too tired to think. In the back of his mind, he was vaguely aware of the others following him down, yet all of his attention was given to taking one more step.

Thick drops of blood oozed from the heel of his shoe, and each step left a slick stain on the rung of the ladder. The pain was unbearable.

As he made his way, Jack began to cry. All he wanted was to sit on his mother's lap and have her tell him everything was going to be all right.

She can't be dead! The thought rang in his head. *Mrs. Dumphry is wrong. I will go back to Ballylesson, and I'll save her!*

As he stepped down yet another rung, his feet slipped from the ladder. Far too exhausted to hold on a moment longer, he fell backward. But very quickly, he landed on his back on the hard, cold ground. Jack had been climbing for more than five hours and had finally made it. All thought left him as he gasped for breath and stared upward into the never-ending darkness.

Shortly after Jack's short fall to the bottom, the rest of the group arrived safely. The pain had become overwhelming. No matter how he positioned his body, the agony would not lessen. He whimpered as Arthur knelt and fumbled in the dark for Jack's hand. He held it tightly.

"We made it, Jack!" Arthur gasped, still breathing heavy from the climb. "Mrs. Dumphry said you would be healed when we reached the bottom! And we're here now, so it won't be long."

The air at the bottom of the ladder was far colder than it had been at the top, yet Jack didn't feel it. All he felt was pain. It was no longer just in his leg—his entire body was on fire. He closed his eyes as agony engulfed him.

"You did well, child. You did very well." Mrs. Dumphry sounded both concerned and relieved. Jack opened his eyes to see his ancient teacher kneeling over him with a torch in her hand. "You have reached the end and needn't take another step. You will soon be healed."

As he looked into Mrs. Dumphry's eyes, Jack felt the world spinning around him.

Mrs. Dumphry stepped away and began whirling the torch in a strange and intricate pattern. Faster and faster it spun, sending sparks flying.

"An soilsiú!" Mrs. Dumphry screamed the strange words into the vast darkness, spinning the torch even faster.

"Caith solas ar." This time her voice seemed to be amplified somehow, sounding a little louder than before.

Mrs. Dumphry became perfectly still as she held the torch parallel to the ground. When she let go and stepped back, the torch did not fall, but stayed where it was.

"Teacht chun solais!" This time Mrs. Dumphry only whispered the words, yet they sounded like thunder.

When the final word escaped her lips, the torch began to spin furiously as it rose high into the air. Arthur and Alexia craned their necks as it lifted higher and higher. Even Jack kept his eyes open, captivated by the strange sight. As it rose, fire leaped from the torch, seeming alive as it rocketed out in every direction, spider-webbing through the air. And though most of the fire was sprawling out and upward, some plummeted back to the ground.

Whenever the fire struck something solid, it exploded, sending thousands of multicolored sparks raining down. And for a moment, just before Jack lost consciousness, he saw something so magnificent it took his breath away.

Chapter 20

THE UNDERGROUND CITY IN THE SKY

As Jack opened his eyes, he screamed in pain. He was lying in a large bed in a room he didn't recognize and clutching at his bare chest. He gasped, feeling as if someone had touched him with a firebrand. He looked down to see a burn in the shape of a half moon on his chest, directly over his heart. It was red and puffy and felt tender to the touch.

"How did that happen?" Jack moaned as he carefully prodded the skin around the burn. Yet even as he looked at it, the swelling subsided and the burn settled into a scar, suddenly looking as if it had been there for months. When he touched it again, there was no pain.

What was that? he wondered, throwing his legs over the side of the bed. Very carefully, he stretched his wounded leg. Although he felt a small twinge of pain, it was nothing like it had been before. The leg looked quite bruised, and though he could see the teeth marks from the Oriax bite, the blackness was gone, and it was hardly swollen at all.

When Jack's eyes landed on the table in the corner of the room, he grinned. It was filled with a small mountain of food, and he was absolutely starving. Wearing only his smallclothes, Jack stood and tested his leg. It felt almost as good as new. He quickly walked over and stuffed a large piece of warm bread into his mouth. Someone must have just been here.

Over the next several minutes, he devoured the most amazing cheeses, chicken, and beef. He gulped a full pitcher of milk, then spread thick strawberry jam onto more bread, stuffing it down. When he reached for more cheese, he was astounded to see he had eaten absolutely all of the food on the table. It should have been enough for five people, yet he still felt slightly hungry.

Grinning happily, he walked over to a large cupboard and opened it, searching for his clothes. Jack froze. On the shelf was a sword. Its handle was wrapped in black leather, and on its pommel was the head of a roaring lion. The sword was sheathed in a black scabbard covered in golden scrollwork. He had seen this sword before. Lying next to the sword was a solid black cloak, and even before he unfolded the stormy-blue shirt, he knew he would find intricate golden threadwork sewn onto both shoulders.

Jack just stood there, holding the clothes and feeling as if he were in a dream. The last time he'd seen them, he'd been wearing them. Or rather, another Jack had been wearing them. Jack had been lying on the ground with the Shadowfog flooding over him. He'd been lying next to the other Jack who'd been wearing these clothes. What was it the other Jack had said? He closed his eyes, trying to remember the exact words. The black-clad Jack had been weeping uncontrollably.

"You have to listen to them, do you hear me? You have to listen! It's you who kills them. You kill them all, don't you understand? Mother, the town, the city of Agartha—it's all your fault!" And then the sword-bearing Jack had tried to choke him to death.

He shuddered at the memory. He'd convinced himself it had been a bad dream or maybe a trick of the Shadowfog. But he knew now that it had been real. "I wish Father or Parker were here," he said quietly. He needed to talk to someone. And besides Arthur and maybe Alexia, he didn't know who to trust. Parker and Father must know about Mother by now. He pushed the image of his mother lying on a sea of green grass from his mind.

"You're awake!"

Jack was startled. He jumped high and spun around to see Arthur and Alexia standing in the doorway. Alexia took one look at him, blushed furiously, and turned around. Only then did Jack realize he was standing in his smallclothes, holding the pile of clothing and the sword. Jack also blushed as he quickly ducked behind the cupboard and changed into his new clothes.

"I'm sorry! I didn't know you were ... I'm sorry!" Alexia sounded horrified.

Arthur grinned as he walked into the room. "You aren't going to believe this place, Jack. It's amazing! And the people—I've never met anyone like them. And there are giants here! Real giants."

Jack quickly laced up his strange new shirt as Arthur's words washed over him. His eyes lingered on the black sword. He didn't care what Arthur thought was amazing. He didn't care about any of it. His leg was mostly healed, and he could leave. He could finally go back to Ballylesson. Something about seeing the sword and putting on the clothes made everything feel even more real. All of the fear and heartache, all the running and pain he'd experienced became overwhelming as his fingers tightened around the pommel of the sword.

"Take me to Mrs. Dumphry," Jack demanded.

"Wow! Who gave you that?" Arthur pointed excitedly at the sword.

"Arthur! Take me to Mrs. Dumphry," Jack repeated. The last thing he wanted to do was talk about the sword.

"Mrs. Dumphry is meeting with the Council of Seven," Arthur replied quickly. "They're in the Council Chamber and won't be finished for hours yet. Besides, they don't allow visitors in the Council Chamber. They've been meeting every day since we got here. But, Jack, you have to see it! The entire city was built underground! Yet it's not like any city I've ever heard of. Its incredible!

"Oh!" Arthur slapped his forehead. "You will never believe who arrived last night! I don't know how to explain her, really, but I've never imagined anyone so beautiful. She's not human, Jack. Wild said she's a Sephari, as if that explains anything."

Jack tried to break in, but Arthur bulldozed over him. "And guess what? There's a school here! It's not like our school—here they learn how to be awake. Or that's what they call it. But everyone in the school is like me! All of them have had the scales, or whatever, fall off. They let me join them for the last few weeks. I haven't learned much yet, but—"

Jack interrupted angrily. "How long have we been here?"

"You were really sick," Arthur responded without answering his question. "Even Miel didn't seem sure she'd be able to heal you, and they say she is the best healer to ever live." Arthur put his hands in his pockets. "You didn't move for days—"

"Arthur! How long?" Jack interrupted him.

"Three months," Arthur said nervously. "You've been in bed for three months. There's nothing we could have done. Everyone on the Council agreed with Mrs. Dumphry. They said if we went back, all we would do was hurt everyone we loved."

Jack sat on the bed fighting back tears.

"Alexia tried to escape," Arthur continued quietly. "She's tried to run away three times now, to get back to Ballylesson. She wanted to … to bury your mother. But the city is impossible to leave."

Jack stared at the sword in his hands as Alexia turned slowly, peeking to make sure he'd gotten dressed. When she saw him fully clothed, she turned to face him, looking grim.

"We're trapped," she said hopelessly. "They don't even have to watch us. The city is all bridges, and no matter how hard I search, I can't find the way out."

Jack looked at Alexia. She was older, stronger, and wiser to the ways of the world than he was. If she couldn't escape, how could he?

"Take me to Mrs. Dumphry," he said again.

"They don't let anyone into their Council," Alexia said bitterly. "I've tried."

"They've been meeting every day for hours and hours," Arthur added. "I think they can't agree on something."

"They won't even tell us what's going on," Alexia said. "They're treating us like children!"

Jack thought for a moment, then stood. "Apparently, you and I aren't just children"—he smiled bitterly—"we are the Children of Prophecy. And today we are going to speak to this Council."

Alexia barked a laugh, but when she met Jack's eyes, she gave a wicked smile. "Okay, then, let's do it."

Arthur paled slightly but stayed silent. The three children marched out of the room, Jack carrying the scabbarded sword. As they exited the chamber, he stopped and stared in awe. They were standing on a small bridge. It was just wide enough for them to walk side by side. As far as he could see were bridges, both large and small, sprawling out in every direction.

Although they looked to be made of dark stone, they sparkled as if something shiny had been placed inside the stone. There were thousands of these strange pathways in the sky. Above and below, they stretched out as far as he could see, each bridge leading to a separate chamber. Some of the chambers seemed far larger than Jack's house, and others appeared as small as a closet. Everything was made of the same sparkling stone as the bridges.

Jack turned slowly. He didn't bother to try to count the bridges. The strangest thing about this place was the light. Jack was pretty sure they were still underground, but it wasn't as dark as a cavern would be. The strange bluish-white light illuminating everything was obviously not the light of the sun. He didn't know where it came from, but he could see quite far.

There were no buildings or towers or halls or cathedrals, just bridges leading to chambers leading to more bridges. Jack felt sure that if one bridge or chamber were to collapse, the entire city would come crashing down. Many of the bridges looked small and delicate, while others were much too thick and heavy to span as far as they did. Was he truly meant to walk across them?

As far as he could tell, the chambers weren't held up by anything other than the bridges. And the bridges weren't held up by anything other than the chambers. Often a chamber would have six or more bridges leading to it, and sometimes there would be just one. Jack walked to the edge of the bridge and looked down. He was so high he couldn't see the ground. If he were to fall off, he would continue falling until he either hit one of the bridges or chambers or the ground he supposed must be somewhere far below.

Cascading between many of the bridges were waterfalls. The water came from somewhere far above and flowed to somewhere far below. Many of the waterfalls flowed directly through the chambers.

Arthur grinned, motioning toward the city. "It was built by the giants thousands of years ago. They say it took three thousand years to complete. I told you there are giants here, right? Real giants! I have only seen three so far, but Andreal is one of them, and he's on the Council. He scares me, Jack. He's huge and has a temper something fierce! Aias told me they built the city this way so that wherever you are, you can always see who's coming long before they arrive. If an enemy attacks, they'll never be able to sneak up on you."

Arthur slapped his forehead yet again before continuing. "And do you remember Aias? The man with the scar over his eye who helped bring us here? It's so weird, Jack, but I'm sure that he and Mrs. Dumphry are in love. Can you imagine that?" Arthur scrunched up his face, obviously disgusted.

Alexia rolled her eyes at Arthur before addressing Jack. "The city works as a maze of sorts. This is why it's been so hard to escape. Even if I could find out where the exits are, I'd have to learn the correct paths to get there. And there are thousands of them! It took me a month before I could come and visit you without getting lost."

Jack shook his head in wonder. "This doesn't change anything," he said, giving Arthur a nervous glance. "You're sure it will hold us?"

Arthur nodded enthusiastically. "They say it's far stronger than steel, but I still hold my breath when I get to the middle parts."

As the children began walking up the bridge, Jack saw what made the stone sparkle. It almost looked like there were veins of gold and silver in the stone beneath his feet. He also thought he saw diamonds, but he was sure he must be wrong. Who would place gold, silver, and diamonds in something you walk on?

Arthur grinned again when he saw Jack's gaze. "They say most of the world is sleepwalking through life. That those who have not yet awakened—that's what they call us by the way, the Awakened—they say those who have not yet awakened place importance on things that have no importance."

Arthur was in awe as he spoke. "In the real world, gold and jewels are meaningless. They are simply tools, like stone or dirt. Can you imagine? They use diamonds to make paving stones! They say it makes them almost impossible to destroy. To hear them talk is really quite amazing!"

As they neared the center of the bridge, Jack realized he was holding his breath. Surely the entire thing was about to collapse. He was so intent on the bridge that he nearly ran into Wild, who was approaching from the opposite direction.

"It's good to see you awake, Jack." Wild grinned. "No one was sure how long you'd be out. But I know Mrs. Dumphry wanted you to stay in bed until you have your strength back."

Jack offered Wild a tight smile. "I'm not going to sit around and do nothing. We're on our way to see Mrs. Dumphry."

"She's meeting with the Council, and they won't let you in," Wild told Jack. "They don't like to be interrupted. Besides, when they hear you're awake, I'm sure they'll come to your chamber soon enough."

"We aren't going to wait, Wild. I don't care what they want." Jack tried his best to make his voice hard. He was frantic. *How could I have been sleeping for three months?*

After a moment, Wild nodded. "All right, I suppose I'll come along as well, then."

All four children began walking down the other side of the bridge. Jack lost count of how many bridges they crossed over. Each bridge led to a very different type of chamber. Sometimes they walked directly through a chamber to a bridge on the other side, and other times there was a walkway around the outside, leading to another bridge. Jack was interested to see men, women, and children walking along the bridges and going about their daily business. When he saw the animals, he gasped.

"The Awakened call them Clear Eyes," Arthur said excitedly. "The animals are just like us. Well, like the rest of us, not like you and Alexia, I suppose. But when they are born, animals also have scales over their eyes. And when the scales fall off, they are awakened to the real world. They're not tame and they don't let you pet them, but I've heard it said that they will fight the Shadow Souled as fiercely as any human!"

Jack could barely believe it. There were almost as many animals as there were humans. He searched the surrounding bridges to see three bears, two rhinos, an elephant, and a moose. He noticed that most of the people steered clear of the animals, but they didn't seem particularly afraid of them. The underground city was a magical place, and at any other time Jack would have been desperate to explore it. But right now all he wanted was to talk to Mrs. Dumphry.

Some of the chambers contained shops, while others held gardens, though every chamber was only a single room. Every person they passed stopped to stare at them.

"Why are they staring like that?" Jack asked in a whisper.

"They think we are special." Alexia shook her head irritably. "They've been staring at me since I arrived, but I don't think they believed you existed until now. It doesn't matter what you say, or if you yell at them, they just keep staring and whispering."

"They think one of you is evil," Arthur added. "They say one of you will try to destroy the Awakened and the other will try to save them, but they don't know who will do what, so they are all rather confused about it. I think that's what the Council's been meeting about since we got here."

Alexia and Jack stopped as Arthur and Wild kept walking. After a moment, it seemed Arthur realized his friends weren't with him. When he turned back and saw the looks on their faces, he raised his hands. "I didn't say I believed them! But I've been talking to some of them, and that's what they're saying."

"You need to stop talking to them." Alexia had a dangerous look in her eyes.

"Don't get mad at me. I'm on your side, remember?" Arthur replied.

"What else do they say?" Jack didn't like the idea of everyone in this city thinking they knew something about him.

"That's it, I swear," Arthur said. "And I've told them they're wrong, but they've got a bloomin' prophecy, so they won't listen."

"Let's go." Jack was growing more frustrated by the second, and his leg was beginning to stiffen. Besides that, he was starting to get hungry again. He barely noticed his surroundings as they crossed over several more bridges and through many more chambers. The longer they walked, the darker his thoughts became.

Over an hour later they were standing in front of a large door and Jack was breathing heavily. The bridge leading to the Council Chamber was the widest they'd crossed, wide enough for ten horses to walk side by side. Lying next to the door were a number of impressive-looking weapons: two large, half-mooned axes, a long sword, two short swords, a staff, some sort of barbed pole, and a sling.

"Well, here we are," Wild said, looking around nervously.

"I've walked in twice now," Alexia growled. "The first time, they just forced me out. The second time …," she trailed off, blushing slightly. Both Wild and Arthur blushed as well, being sure not to look at Alexia. Whatever happened, she was clearly both furious and embarrassed about it.

"If you are really going in, you should leave your sword here," Wild told them. "Weapons aren't allowed in the Council Chamber."

Jack ignored Wild. Keeping a tight grip on the sword, he took a deep breath, stepped forward, and shoved open the doors.

Chapter 21

THE BEZELS MAR

Six faces turned to look as Jack, Alexia, and Arthur stalked into the Council Chamber. Wild had stayed outside, not wanting to be on the receiving end of the Council's wrath.

From the outside, the chamber looked no different from the others Jack had seen. Yet as he walked in, his eyes immediately darted to the walls. Every inch from floor to ceiling was covered in tapestries unlike any Jack had seen before. They were impossibly intricate, and as he walked across the chamber, Jack felt as if the pictures were moving with him, showing different scenes depending on where he stood. On the opposite side of the chamber was a large silvery structure of interlocking rings. It reached almost as high as the ceiling and made a sphere of sorts.

Seven Council members were seated on cushions around a pool of blue light in the center of the chamber. The light bubbled like water, and every time a bubble popped, a tiny burst of colored light exploded outward. Jack immediately recognized Mrs. Dumphry and Aias in the ring of people, but it was the others who drew his eye.

Next to Mrs. Dumphry was a giant. He was half again larger than any man Jack had ever seen. He had long, braided hair and a very thick beard. The hair on the top of his head was so red it was almost orange, while his beard was the color of pitch. "That's Andreal," Arthur whispered. Andreal wore a thick leather coat and a black kilt with gray trim. Jack could barely believe his eyes. He'd never believed giants were real. They'd just been characters in fairy tales and bedtime stories!

Next to Andreal was a girl who didn't look to be much older than Jack. She had auburn hair and eyes the shape and color of almonds. She wore loose-fitting trousers tucked in at the tops of her boots, which laced up to the knees. "That's Sage," Arthur whispered as he pointed to the girl. "Next to her is Miel, then Honi. Miel is the one who healed you."

Miel had olive skin and was quite beautiful. Her cloak was covered in so much golden threadwork it might as well have been made of solid gold. Honi was an old man with a thick gray beard that hung below his belt. He wore a plain brown cloak and had piercing eyes.

"And the one in the middle is Elion," Arthur breathed.

The seventh member of the council was smaller than the rest and had her back to the door. At first, Jack struggled to see her. All he could see was her long golden hair, which seemed to be floating in midair. As he looked closer, he realized she was wearing a cloak of some sort. The cloak somehow matched the color of the chamber.

Jack found his eyes wanting to slide past the woman, and he had to concentrate to keep them focused. Elion was the only one who didn't turn to look as Jack and the others walked in.

"Child, it is good to see you awake," Mrs. Dumphry said. "But you cannot be here. We will come to your chamber soon enough. As for the two of you"—she fixed Alexia and Arthur with a cold stare— "rest assured we will speak of this later. Perseverance and stupidity may attend the same ball, but wisdom only dances with one. You may all leave, now."

Jack broke his eyes away from the cloaked woman and turned to meet Mrs. Dumphry's gaze.

"No," Jack said calmly. He didn't scream, and he didn't feel like crying. A cold rage burned inside him. He had come to deliver a message, and nothing else mattered.

"Young Mr. Staples," Mrs. Dumphry chided, "you will listen or—"

"I'm done listening." Jack's voice was cold steel. "It's time for you to listen. You are going to answer our questions, and then we are leaving this city. If you won't take us back to Ballylesson, we'll go on our own, but we're not staying here."

"Let him speak." The golden-haired woman stood and turned to face Jack and the others. As she turned, she pushed her dizzying cloak back so it hung behind her. She was slim, only a little taller than Jack, and she was definitely not human. Her ears were pointed, and her milky white skin sparkled when she moved. Her eyes were large and astonishingly bright and seemed to gather the light of the room, changing color even as she looked at him. Human or not, Jack thought she was absolutely stunning.

"It's you," Jack exclaimed in awe. "You were in my dream! I saw you standing next to my mother."

"I wondered how much you would remember." Her voice was melodic and had a dreamlike quality to it. Stepping forward, she bowed her head. "Yes, Jack, I was there. My name is Elion, and I am pleased to meet you for the second time." She smiled warmly.

"But ... how? It was a dream. I don't understand."

"I think you do," she responded.

Jack opened his mouth to tell her he didn't know what she was talking about, but instead he said, "It wasn't a dream. It was real."

Elion nodded her affirmation. "Yes, it was real."

"But how?"

"The question is not how, Jack, but when? When were you there?"

Jack blinked in confusion.

"When I first met you, on the night you arrived in the room that would someday become your bedroom, you announced yourself by name. Both your mother and I were as confused as you. You see, back then you had not yet been born. In a way, it was quite amusing." Elion chuckled, her laugh sounding like a beautiful song. "It was you who told your mother what to name you."

Jack wanted to sit. He shook his head slightly but knew she was right. His mother hadn't recognized him, and it had been far too real to be a dream.

"Although I don't fully understand it," Elion continued, "you have the ability, at least in a small way, to walk through time."

Even if Jack hadn't believed her, his clothing and the sword in his hand were proof enough.

"Time has given you different rules than the rest of us. I will do my best to help you learn those rules, but it will take … time." Elion smiled yet again.

Jack didn't know what to think. There was simply too much to take in.

Elion stepped forward and placed her hands on Jack's shoulders, and as she did, her eyes gathered even more light. "Jack, I am happy to tell you all I know. I will answer every question you have, so long as I know the answer. But first, I need you to tell me something. Will you do that for me?"

Jack nodded.

"I need you to tell me what you saw when you looked at the Masc Tinneas"

"What is a Masc Tinneas?" he asked numbly.

"When you looked at the papers that were on my desk, child, the map," Mrs. Dumphry prompted. "Tell us what you saw."

Suddenly wary, Jack stepped back, breaking from Elion's grip. The question scared him. He'd tried to forget what happened in the schoolhouse that night. But as he looked into Elion's eyes, he remembered his mother's words. They had been standing outside in the deep snow and howling wind. She'd held him close and told him that he would soon meet Elion and that he could "trust her above all."

"I saw someone who looked a little like you," Jack said, addressing Elion, "except he was much taller and so bright I could barely look at him. But he had your eyes and ears, and his skin sparkled like yours. He was standing on the side of a great mountain." Jack trembled as he remembered. "I heard him talking to someone, or maybe he was talking to himself, but I couldn't see because he was too bright. He said his name was Belial, and he was planning to attack someone. He said"—Jack shuddered at the memory—"he said he would unseat the Author. And when he started to sing, the whole world shook."

Elion's eyes widened, gathering even more light and shifting to a transparent white. "Until now," Elion said, "there were very few in this world who would know that name. I am one of them." Elion turned to address the other Council members, and as she did, her body vanished to Jack's eyes as the strange cloak reflected the room.

"Today, Belial goes by another name. You know him as the Assassin."

The room surged into motion as all but Mrs. Dumphry and Aias leaped to their feet and reached for weapons that were not there. And all but Mrs. Dumphry and Aias looked at Jack as if he had been transformed into a rabid wolf.

"It be the boy! He be the one who'll destroy us!" the giant shouted.

"The Author will protect us," Miel whispered.

Even Arthur and Alexia seemed uncertain.

"Sit down." Elion didn't scream or speak loudly, but one by one the Council sat, looking slightly embarrassed; all except Andreal.

"Ye hear the boy, Elion," the giant rumbled. "He be condemning heself with he own words!" His accent was strange, and Jack had trouble understanding him. "It be clear, he be the child who'll destroy us!"

Elion took a step toward him. "I also know the name Belial. Does that make me your enemy?" Her eyes blazed a translucent red. "Would you condemn me?"

"It be far different, and ye know it!" the giant boomed.

Elion didn't bother to answer but turned to face Jack. "What you witnessed happened before Time was born. Belial was once the greatest being ever created. He was named the Lord of Harmony, and when he sang, all creation stopped to listen. In the end, it was his pride that was his downfall. He believed he could unseat the Author." Elion stepped closer. "Jack, I believe what you witnessed was the start of the war—the very birth of evil."

Jack didn't know how to respond. When he looked at Arthur and Alexia, both were staring as if they'd never seen him before.

"But tell me," Elion continued, "what happened next? There is something you are keeping from me; I can feel it."

Jack's throat caught.

"Do not fear. I am a friend, and I will protect you with my life."

After a moment Jack nodded. "When I touched the desk, something happened. I don't know, but I think I was somehow on the mountain with him."

As he spoke, an uncertain look entered Elion's eyes.

"He ... he spoke to me. He said that ... that he had great plans for me." This was the hardest part for Jack to say, because it was this that scared him more than anything. "And then he touched me, here." Jack's hand went to his heart.

"Jack." Elion tensed. "Let me see exactly where he touched you."

Jack slowly pulled his shirt down to reveal a half-moon scar. "It wasn't there before," he said numbly. "It's what woke me up just a little while earlier. My chest started to burn, and then this appeared."

Elion turned to the Council. "Sage, sound the alarm and rally the Awakened! The city is under siege!"

Sage looked at Elion in confusion.

"Go, now!" Elion's eyes blazed a fiery orange.

"Yes, Elion," Sage said as she dashed from the chamber.

The rest of the Council looked as confused as Jack felt. Even Mrs. Dumphry seemed uncertain.

"The Assassin has marked Jack." Elion's face was stone, her eyes a stormy blue.

"But the boy has been here for months now," Mrs. Dumphry said. "How is it the Assassin is only coming now?"

"The mark on Jack's chest is a Beezles Mar. I have not seen one since time before time. A Beezles Mar can stay invisible for long periods. Yet once it appears, the one who gave the mark can follow it like a beacon. It can remove it, but right now we must prepare for battle. Have no doubt; the Assassin will be leading this army. If he is not here already, he will be in Agartha within the hour."

From somewhere outside a bell began to toll.

"NO," Andreal screamed, jumping to his feet once again. "The boy, he must die! Can ye no see it, Elion? It be he who'll destroy us! The prophecy be clear! If we kill him now, maybe we blind the Assassin before it be too late!"

From outside the Council Chamber, many more bells began to sound as Elion turned toward Andreal. "I warn you," she said, her eyes turning an icy blue, "if you touch a hair on this boy's head, it will be you who loses your life!"

"But he be bringing the Assassin! Ye must see it! What more do ye need to be hearing?"

"Tell me." Elion was angry now. "What are the other names for the Assassin? Is he not also the Father of Lies, the Deceiver, the Imposter? Yes, he followed Jack here, but the boy did not lead him!"

"But the prophecy!"

"Enough!" Elion's eyes turned black, and as she stepped toward Andreal, her golden hair began to shine and rise from her shoulders. "I have warned you, Andreal. Do not cross me," she said dangerously.

The giant lifted his hands in surrender, taking a step back and paling slightly.

When she turned to Jack, Elion's hair was back to normal and her eyes settled to a deep green. "Jack, when we have more time, I will answer every question you have. You have my word. But I need you to tell me one last thing right now. Before you walk through time, do you hear music? Do you hear the ringing of bells?"

Jack nodded.

"No matter what happens next, when you hear the ring of Time, I need you to try and shut it out. You must not listen to her call, do you understand?"

Outside the chamber, from somewhere far in the distance, something roared. Yet it wasn't the roar of an Oriax—it was much deeper and infinitely more terrifying.

Jack glanced fearfully toward the door. Everything was happening so fast. "What do you mean by 'shut it out'? What is it?"

"It was music that birthed Time. When you hear her call, when you hear the ring of Time, you must not listen, you must not embrace it! Now that you know you're not dreaming, it is far too dangerous to go back. You must not time travel without more understanding of what you are doing. You could change everything." Elion stepped even closer. "I need you to hear me, Jack. If you try and go back, the Assassin can follow. He cannot walk through Time as you can, but he can follow where you go. And if you go back, one wrong move could destroy everything."

Something exploded nearby, and screams began to sound from outside the chamber. Everyone turned to look toward the open door as howls, gurgles, growls, and shrieks grew ever louder.

"We are out of time." Elion placed a hand on Jack's shoulder. "The sword you carry is not a normal sword. It is named Ashandar, and it once belonged to the greatest swordsman on earth. The black blade is both teacher and tool. To use it well you must surrender to it." Elion smiled. "The Author be with you, Jack Staples."

Elion turned to Alexia. "Alexia, I was there the day you were born. It was I who kept you hidden from the Assassin. Your Soulprint is as powerful as Jack's. And when this battle is over, I will answer all of your questions as well."

Alexia stared at Elion with wide eyes.

"You knew about her and you didn't tell us?" Mrs. Dumphry was shocked. "You didn't tell me?"

"I do not answer to you," Elion chided. "It had to be done. Now, I must go before it is too late. If the Author allows it, I will lead the Assassin away. Mrs. Dumphry, Aias, whatever happens, keep them safe. If we cannot protect Jack and Alexia, all is lost."

Mrs. Dumphry nodded grimly. "The Assassin himself won't get past us."

"Let us pray it does not come to that. The rest of you, come with me," Elion said. As she strode from the chamber, she pulled her cloak tightly around her, almost vanishing completely.

Chapter 22

THE BATTLE OF AGARTHA

All three children sat huddled against the back wall of the Council Chamber listening to the muted sounds of battle. Mrs. Dumphry, Aias, and Wild had left, ordering them to stay inside no matter what they heard. Alexia had protested, but Mrs. Dumphry merely shut the door in her face.

The children jumped as something roared from just outside. A large explosion immediately followed, and the chamber shook violently as dust rained down.

"It's all going to collapse," Arthur said, wide-eyed. "The bridges, the chambers, all of it!" Jack had been thinking the same thing. It seemed to him that if just one bridge or chamber collapsed, the entire city would crumble.

"I brought him here," Jack whispered. "The Assassin followed me." His finger traced the scar over his heart.

Arthur's eyes stayed glued to the ceiling as he spoke. "It's not your fault. You heard Elion; how could you have—"

"NO." Mrs. Dumphry's voice was muffled from outside the door. "You will not have them!" Another great boom shook the chamber. A moment later the ceiling near the door exploded, sending stones flying in every direction.

All three children shielded themselves as shards of stone and diamond rained down. The ceiling and half of the front wall had been destroyed, opening a window into the sky. Above the chamber was a monstrous creature. Its wings and body were covered in golden-black scales, and the beast had the look of both lion and lizard. It was enormous. Its claws were vicious razors and its eyes burning flames. The winged creature had a mane of black fire, and when it roared, the chamber shook.

The mammoth beast breathed a stream of molten fire down on the chamber's entrance. And though she was hidden from sight, it seemed as if Mrs. Dumphry was the cause of its rage. Sprays of white flame shot upward, striking the lizard-like creature in the chest as it bellowed in rage.

"We can't wait here any longer," Alexia shouted as lightning exploded across the sky, striking chamber, bridge, and creature alike. "We have to help!"

All three children now stood with their backs pressed hard against the far wall. Jack nodded, though he had no idea how they were meant to help. Only then did he realize he was still gripping the black-bladed sword, Ashandar.

"Are you crazy?" Arthur shouted. "What can you possibly do against that?"

Alexia stepped forward and began swinging her sling. "I can fight," she said grimly.

"And so can I." Jack buckled Ashandar around his waist, drawing it awkwardly. He was surprised to see that the blade was even blacker than the hilt. For some reason, when Arthur saw the blade, his eyes grew wide, and he looked even sicker than before. Yet Jack had no time to ask him what was wrong.

As they ran toward the door, a bolt of lightning thundered behind them, crumbling the back wall. The moment the wall dropped away, an Oriax with the head and shoulders of a baboon and the body and wings of an eagle landed inside the room. Before the beast could think to attack, a stone struck it between the eyes, killing it instantly.

Behind them, the door burst open, Wild sprinting in. His shoulder was bleeding and his face was smudged with soot. Just outside the door, Aias lay facedown on the bridge with his left arm ending at the elbow. Mrs. Dumphry stood over him, sending steady streams of fire upward.

"We need to go!" Wild's eyes were ablaze. "She won't be able to hold it off much longer." Running to the edge of the chamber where the wall had disintegrated, Wild looked down. A short distance below was another bridge. "We'll have to jump," he shouted, turning to Alexia. "Can you make it?"

Alexia rolled her eyes, then sprang forward, somersaulting through the air and down to the bridge. Wild grimaced, glancing at Jack and Arthur. "We all jump on the count of three."

"I don't think I can make it!" Arthur cried.

"Yes you can!" Jack shouted, placing a hand on his shoulder. "You have to!"

Arthur met Jack's eyes for a moment, then nodded.

"One," Wild yelled.

"Two," Jack and Wild screamed together as another wall exploded behind them.

"Three!" they shouted. Wild and Arthur sprinted forward, leaped high, and landed safely on the bridge below. Only when they looked back did they realize Jack wasn't with them. He was standing at the edge of the chamber with Ashandar in his hands.

"I have to go back!" he yelled. "I have to save them, to change it! It's my fault they're here! But I can save them!"

"No, Jack!" Wild screamed from below. "It's too dangerous; you have to jump!"

Without another word, Jack turned and walked away.

Alexia watched Jack disappear with a sinking feeling in her stomach. *What does he think he's doing?* Something pulled at the corner of her vision, and she turned to see a Shadule landing on the bridge a short distance away.

She immediately sent a stone flying at the creature's head. Yet the Shadule moved lazily aside as it hurtled past. This Shadule was different than the other one Alexia had seen; it had a long scar that began above its right eye and ran all the way down to its pale chest. As the creature's wings melted into its body, the scar became even more pronounced.

The creature sneered as it glided toward Alexia. "Do you see this?" It pointed at the scar. "Your father gave it to me on the day I killed him. And today, I will take my revenge!"

Alexia stopped. Until this moment Wild, Arthur, and Alexia had been backing away from the creature. But when she heard its words, something inside her snapped. *What? This creature killed Father?* Although she couldn't make sense of it, Alexia didn't care what she had to do. She was going to kill this Shadule.

Jack knew what he needed to do. It was clear. Elion's words echoed in his mind: *"It was music that birthed Time. When you hear her call, when you hear the ring of Time, you must not listen, you must not embrace it! Now that you know you're not dreaming, it is far too danger-ous to go back ... You could change everything."*

I can change everything! he realized. Just before Wild and Arthur jumped from the chamber, Jack had made his decision. He was done running. *If I am truly special, if I'm meant to help save the world ... then why not now?* He could save his mother.

He could save Ballylesson, and he could save Agartha. He could change all of it.

Until now Jack had only traveled through time accidentally. But he thought he might understand how it happened. Each time he'd gone back, his life had been threatened or he'd been experiencing something overwhelming or terrifying. And each time, he'd heard the ringing of bells just before he went back.

"Now," he said to himself, "all I need is to be terrified." As he turned and looked at the city of Agartha, it wasn't hard to feel fear. Bridges and chambers crumbled all around as creatures more evil than those of his worst nightmares fought against the citizens of Agartha. Yet where was the music? Why couldn't he hear the bells?

Turning toward the entrance, Jack watched Mrs. Dumphry send another spray of fire up at the mammoth creature. Flapping its wings, the mighty beast roared as fire exploded against its chest. The beast breathed its own molten fire down on Mrs. Dumphry. But just as it was about to strike, the fire exploded against the shield of blue light that appeared around his ancient teacher.

As he stepped out to get a closer look, the lion-like beast spotted him. It roared loudly and dove toward the bridge leading to the chamber. When the creature landed, it began to contort as it shrank inward. Jack watched in amazement as it transformed into the shape of a man.

Jack recognized him. Although he had changed, he was sure it was the same being he'd seen on the mountain. It was Belial, the Lord of Harmony. It was the Assassin, the Father of Evil. As the Assassin walked forward, a dark light emanated from him—a darkness so bright it threatened to blind the world. The Assassin's eyes were deep caverns of fire, and his skin sparkled like diamonds.

"You!" He pointed at Mrs. Dumphry. "You have interfered in my plans for too long!" Though his voice was still musical, it was jarring and held no beauty. Behind him, the city of Agartha burned, and the Assassin's hordes fought the army of the Awakened. For just a moment the Assassin's gaze shifted to Jack who stood a few paces behind Mrs. Dumphry.

His teacher turned to see what the creature had looked at, and when she saw Jack, her eyes widened in fear. "No!" she screamed. "Run, child! You are not ready to face him!" As she turned back to face the Assassin, a wall of darkness exploded into her and sent her flying past Jack and through the broken wall to disappear into the darkness.

"No!" Jack screamed as he ran to the edge to search for his teacher. Yet when he looked down, Mrs. Dumphry was gone. When he turned back to the Assassin, Jack had no trouble feeling terrified. All around them a battle raged, yet he barely saw it. The Assassin was striding toward him.

The Assassin was beautiful—even with the blinding darkness, his hair was black, his skin shone like diamonds, and his eyes shifted between caverns of flame and an icy blue. His cloak shimmered when he walked, and, until he spoke, Jack was mesmerized.

"My boy," the Assassin said. "I have been waiting for you since the day I marked you on the mountain." He offered a waxy smile and stopped just a few paces away. For the second time, Jack found himself standing before the Assassin with nowhere to run. He had backed up to the edge of the ruined wall, and one more step would take him over the edge.

"Come with me, and we will finish what we started. Together, you and I will destroy the Awakened!" A look of ecstasy entered his eyes. "I will make you the High Prince of Thaltorose, and we will rule this world!"

"No!" Jack screamed. He lifted his black blade, pointing it at the Assassin's chest. He had no idea how to use it, but it was all he had. "No," he shouted again. "I would never join you! I just want to go home. I don't care about any of it. Just let me go!"

The Assassin's eyes darted hesitantly toward the sword. "You already serve me," he said smoothly. "It was you who brought me here. It is because of you Agartha burns. I have been searching for this city for thousands of years, and you led me here in a matter of months. You already serve me, but if you choose to follow me of your own free will, anything you want will be yours. Power beyond measure, riches, glory! I will make you a king of kings!" The Assassin extended his hand and offered a smile. "Come with me, Jack."

Jack gripped the sword so hard his knuckles turned white. "If you want me"—his voice was as hard as stone—"come and get me." Without another word, he fell back off the edge of the chamber. He didn't know if it would work, but this was his only hope. Perhaps, if he kept the right time and place in his mind, he could get there. As he sped downward, Agartha crumbled around him. And as he fell, he grinned. Somewhere in the distance Jack heard the ring of Time, and he embraced it.

Chapter 23

STRAWBERRIES ON THE FLOOR

The Shadule flowed toward Alexia, yet she never thought of running. This creature claimed to have killed her father! And though she didn't understand it, she didn't care. For more than eight years, Alexia had lived on her own and fended for herself. Her friends had been the beasts of the circus, and she'd had no family to speak of.

"Run!" Wild screamed from behind her. "Don't just stand there. You aren't strong enough!"

Yet Alexia didn't hear. She stalked toward the Shadule with her sling whirling.

From the corner of her eye, she saw someone fall from the wall of the Council Chamber, dropping like a stone. A moment later, a strange being with pale skin and fiery eyes walked to the edge and stepped off, following Jack down.

Yet Alexia didn't have time to think about anything other than the job in front of her. The only thing that mattered now was killing this Shadule.

Jack hit the ground hard, landing flat on his face with the sword Ashandar lying beside him. For a moment he struggled to breathe. His mind was cloudy, and as he opened his eyes, he was confused. *What am I doing in the front yard?*

"What happened?" he mumbled. Yet the instant his eyes landed on the sword, Jack remembered everything.

"I did it!" he whispered excitedly as he jumped to his feet. "I'm back!"

As he'd fallen through the air, Jack had kept one thought strong in his mind. It had been the picture of his mother wearing her yellow dress and preparing breakfast. He'd pictured the morning he'd found her body in the yard. Sprinting onto the porch with hope in his heart, Jack shoved the door open and ran into the kitchen.

A frying pan was sitting on the stove with bacon sizzling. His mother wore the yellow dress with her red apron over the top. She was carrying two crockery bowls from the counter over to the table; one was filled with fresh strawberries and the second contained five eggs.

As he entered the kitchen, Jack ran into his mother, sending both bowls flying through the air to shatter on the ground. In a moment of panic, he looked at the strawberries and broken eggs splattered on the floor.

"Jack!" his mother said, gasping. "What is it? What's happened?"

Jack couldn't take his eyes off the broken eggs and crockery. *What's happening?*

Taking one look at his clothes and the sword in his hand, his mother quickly walked him to the front door. "Let's talk outside, my boy. We can't let anyone hear you," she said softly. As she reached the door, she took off her apron and dropped it to the floor.

Jack looked around frantically. On the morning he'd found his mother's body, there had been eggs, strawberries, and broken crockery on the floor. Burnt bacon had been sizzling on the stove and her apron had been lying near the front door.

Although he didn't understand what was happening, it didn't matter. The only clear thought he had was that his mother was alive and he could still save her.

"Jack, tell me what's wrong."

"I need you to leave." Tears poured from his eyes. "You need to go. If you don't, you are going to die any minute now!"

For just a moment, panic entered his mother's eyes. Letting out a long, steady breath, she spoke softly. "I'd hoped to have more time," she whispered. As she dropped to her knees, she drew Jack close. "Jacksie, you will someday learn that death is not something to fear. It's not the end, but just another step in our journey. I cannot run, and you must learn that you can't fix everything. Even with your gift, you cannot save everyone." Her tears reflected the morning sun as she kissed his cheek. "My darling boy, thank you for trying to save me. But you must go now."

Jack couldn't believe it. The only thing in the world that mattered to him was saving his mother, and she wouldn't listen! "Mother, don't you understand? Something evil is coming! I don't know what it is, but it will be here any minute. Please! You must go!"

"I love you more than you could ever know. But my place is here. My time is now."

A distant scream sounded from the direction of Ballylesson. It was soon followed by another and then another. Although they were faint, Jack could also hear roars, screeches, hisses, and gurgles. The Oriax were arriving in the sleepy town.

"Please, Mother." Jack began to sob.

His mother quickly grabbed him by the shoulders. "He is here!" she said. "The Assassin … it's not possible! He has come!" When she looked at Jack, her voice was urgent. "You must run, Jack! Go now before it's too late!"

Jack turned to see a thousand shadowed tentacles slithering out of the forest. The Shadowfog formed a wriggling cloud at the Assassin's feet as he stalked menacingly toward them.

"I won't leave you!" Jack cried. "You have to come! You have to let me save you!"

His mother smiled through teary eyes and whispered, "And who do you think will save you, my darling?" She turned to look toward the upstairs windows of the house. "Who do you think will save Alexia? Both of you are sound asleep in your beds, and if I don't stop him, who will?"

Jack had no words. His throat caught as his chest tightened.

His mother's eyes shifted to the Assassin and then down to the sword in Jack's hand. "I don't know if they've told you, but the black sword has power. It is both teacher and blade, and when you hold it, the Shadowfog cannot see or touch you."

As the Assassin walked toward them, his eyes were locked on Jack. Yet he moved slowly, each step both menacing and mocking. And flowing like an ocean at his feet was the Shadowfog.

With tears in his eyes, Jack hugged his mother fiercely. She hugged him back just as hard. "Ah, my Jack. Not even death can keep me from my children. Now, don't come back here again. You cannot save me. I will always love you." Taking Jack by the shoulders, she turned him around and gave him a push to start him running. And as she turned to face the Assassin, a strong wind began to blow, swirling around her.

Agartha was crumbling. Oriax, Shadule, and many other horrifying creatures wreaked havoc on the majestic city. Yet Alexia barely noticed. Every ounce of her energy was spent staying alive. The Shadule was quicker than any serpent, and all of its energy was focused on her.

Alexia had left Wild and Arthur behind long ago. The silly boys had tried to help her, but if she hadn't lured the Shadule away, she had no doubt they both would be dead by now. So she'd run, leading it away as she leaped from bridge to bridge. The stupid thing thought she was scared, yet all she felt was cold anger.

Somersaulting onto a small bridge barely a pace wide, Alexia sprinted toward a chamber. As she ran, an Oriax landed in front of her, but she didn't slow. The beast never expected the girl with the sling to be dangerous. As her stone struck it between the eyes, she sprinted past, not bothering to watch it fall. Flying through the air just behind her, Alexia could hear the wings of the pursuing Shadule.

If she could just get to the chamber before the Shadule reached her, she would be able to make her move.

Jack ran blindly, tears streaming from his eyes. He had no idea where he was going, but as he reached the path at the back of his house, he stopped and turned around. The Shadowfog had risen high into the air and was boiling like a black cloud. And standing inside the cloud were the Assassin and his mother. His mother stood in the center of the roiling darkness, a mighty wind whirling around her. As she stretched out her hands, a pure, white light exploded from her chest just above her heart.

Boom!

The Assassin staggered as he was momentarily enveloped in brilliant white flames. The Shadowfog shrieked as Jack watched in awe. With all of his attention focused on his mother, he didn't hear the Oriax burst from the trees behind him. A moment before it crashed into him, Killer, the second lion from the circus, was there. The lion roared as it dove at the other beast, bringing it to the ground.

Jack turned to see an Oriax with the head and shoulders of a polar bear and the body of a wildebeest. Killer roared, sinking his teeth into the beast's neck and pinning it to the ground. Yet even as the Oriax howled in pain, it rolled onto its back, freeing itself from the lion's grasp.

Jack watched wide-eyed as Killer glanced back at him and growled, as if to say, "Run!" And with nothing but fear in his heart, Jack ran.

Sprinting the last few paces to the chamber, Alexia stole a quick glance over her shoulder. The Shadule was making its move. Its long arms were outstretched, and its clawed hands nearly close enough to grasp her shoulders.

Perfect! she thought as she sprinted at the chamber and ran straight up the side of the wall. When she'd run a few steps, she lunged and flipped her body around to land on the Shadule's back.

The creature screamed, flapping its wings furiously and rising high into the air. But Alexia held tight, wrapping her arms securely around its neck as it flew ever higher.

Chapter 24

A BOY, A SWORD, AND
A STREET FIGHT

When Jack stumbled onto the main street of Ballylesson, he was horrified. He hadn't realized he was running into town; he'd just been running blindly. A number of the buildings were in flames, and many of the men and women he'd known his whole life had been corralled in the center of town, surrounded by Oriax.

A Shadule stood among the cowering townsfolk, holding Doctor Falvey by the neck a pace above the ground. Cowering at the Shadule's feet were a number of townsfolk, some of them clutching at their eyes as if in pain.

"Where is the Child of Prophecy? Tell me now, and we will leave your pathetic town. If you resist, I will burn it to the ground," the Shadule rattled. "I will kill every last one of you!"

White-hot rage boiled inside of Jack. A few buildings were already wreathed in flames. These were his people; they were his friends, and this evil was here because it was looking for him. Doctor Falvey's legs thrashed, and he began to turn blue.

"Here I am!" Jack screamed.

The Shadule's eyes locked on Jack. It dropped a gasping Doctor Falvey and turned to face the small boy with the sword. One by one the Oriax also turned to face him.

Jack had never been so angry. And somehow, he wasn't afraid anymore. All he felt was rage. "Well, what are you waiting for?" he asked. "Come and get me!" The pommel of the sword warmed. Elion had named the blade Ashandar, and as he held it now, the black blade felt alive in his hands.

"Take him," the creature rasped, "but do not kill him. The master wants the child alive." As one, the Oriax began stalking, slithering, and hopping toward Jack. The townsfolk immediately darted away. Those who clutched at their eyes were helped by the others, and everyone ran into the nearest buildings and locked the doors.

These beasts were the cause of Jack's pain; this evil was the reason for everything that had gone wrong. As the Oriax closed the gap, Jack did … something. His hands burned as the black sword called to him. He focused all his rage, all his sorrow into the blade and moved in a way he'd never moved before. He dove under the haunches of an Oriax with the head of a hyena and the body of a zebra, and as he rolled, he sliced down the center of its belly.

Spinning, Jack dove at an Oriax that was part raccoon and part turtle, twisting Ashandar upward, hitting its mark. As he turned, the five remaining Oriax began to circle him, suddenly cautious. Until now, the Shadule had stood and watched, yet seeing that Jack was not helpless, it dropped to the ground and slithered forward.

Not far off, walking slowly out from the woods, was the Assassin. When the Assassin saw Jack surrounded by the Oriax and the Shadule, he stopped to watch, Shadowfog boiling at his feet. When Jack saw the Assassin, he knew in his heart his mother was dead. Consumed by rage, he screamed and began to flow between the beasts in a gruesome dance. And one by one the Oriax fell to his black-bladed fury.

As Jack turned to face the approaching Shadule, the snakelike creature slowed its approach. Screaming in rage, Jack attacked, charging it as he struck out with Ashandar again and again. Yet the Shadule was viperously quick. Each time Jack's sword came down, the creature slithered aside at the last moment.

The Assassin watched Jack fight the Shadule with a demonic smile. The Shadule was no longer pursuing Jack; it was now trying to flee from the boy with the black blade. Jack gave himself to his anger. He would kill them all, every last Oriax, every last Shadule. He would kill the Assassin himself!

In an attempt to escape, the Shadule leaped through the window of O'flannigans, sending glass flying everywhere. Screaming furiously, Jack dove in behind it. The creature rattled as it slithered away, knocking down shelves and shattering everything in the store as it tried to escape. The Shadule darted out the back door and into the alley. But Jack stayed on its heels, quickly cornering the creature between the alley and the outhouse. And as it turned to face him, the Shadule was backed up to the outhouse door. Horror shone in its pale eyes.

"No!" it cried. "Spare me!" Yet Jack didn't hear it. With only rage in his heart and his hands burning like fire, he stood before the Shadule and screamed.

Jack felt hollow as he spun around and swung Ashandar hard. He closed his eyes as the blade struck flesh, and the creature crumbled. Ashandar had pierced through the outhouse door, and Jack had to yank it free. As he turned to leave, he heard someone whimpering from inside the outhouse and felt suddenly sick to his stomach. *What did I just do? It was begging for mercy and I killed it!* It was a cold thought. He stepped over the dead Shadule and began to shake.

Alexia held tightly to the back of the flying Shadule, her arms wrapped around its neck and her knees clasped to its sides. The creature screamed as it vaulted through the air, its snakelike body writhing and twisting constantly.

If there was one thing Alexia didn't fear, it was heights. No matter how high the creature flew, she kept her wits about her. As they twisted and spun upward, she managed to wrap her sling around its neck. The sling had two purposes. She was able to use it as a kind of reins, as if she were riding a flying horse, while also using it to strangle the creature.

The Shadule snarled as it flew higher. They had left the city far below, and though they were still underground, they were drawing near the earth above.

The creature flipped and twisted suddenly, taking Alexia by surprise as she flew over its head. Yet she held tight to her sling, which was still wrapped securely around the Shadule's neck. The Shadule let out a strangled shriek. Then both girl and creature dropped like stones. Alexia held tightly to her sling as the Shadule, wings fully extended, spiraled down, face-first above her.

Alexia and the Shadule plummeted past bridges and chambers where the Awakened battled the Assassin's hordes. And as they drew near the ground, the creature groaned in pain as its wings slammed against some of the nearby bridges, slowing their descent. Just moments before they landed, Alexia pulled hard on her sling, catapulting the creature down even faster and slowing her fall even more. And as the Shadule passed her in the air, she climbed its body and dove upward. Her crimson cloak swirled above her, catching the wind and billowing out.

Alexia's cloak wasn't nearly enough to stop her fall, but it did slow it a little. And as the creature crashed into the earth, a moment later, Alexia landed on top of it.

Feeling something cold and hollow forming inside his chest, Jack walked out of O'flannigans. His rage had evaporated and was quickly replaced by a bone-deep weariness. As he stepped into the street, he couldn't stop shaking. Jack fell to his knees, utterly exhausted. All of it was a blur. Had he really killed the Oriax and the Shadule? He'd never so much as touched a sword before, but the movements had felt so natural. Yet even though the evil creatures were dead, he didn't feel even the slightest bit better.

As he looked up, Jack was shocked to see the Assassin standing just a few paces away. He waited in the center of the street, watching Jack with admiration in his eyes. At his feet, the Shadowfog slithered and boiled.

"You are a natural killer, Jack." The Assassin's voice was jarring, like two forms of music colliding. "I am proud of you. Only when you give yourself to your rage will you find true power. It is this that makes you strong. We are alike, you and I." The Assassin's smile never reached his eyes.

Jack was fatigued beyond words. His rage was gone, and in its place was nothing. A great void filled him. As he looked down, he saw his hands slick with the milky white blood of the Shadule. He wanted to vomit. Slowly, he stood to his feet. He didn't want to be on his knees in front of this creature.

"I am nothing like you." Jack didn't scream. He didn't have the energy for it. "You killed my mother."

"I may have extinguished her life, but it was you who brought me here. It was you who showed me how to find her."

"No." Jack shook his head in denial. "You are a liar." He swung Ashandar wildly, yet nothing happened. The black blade felt awkward and heavy in his hands.

"My servants have searched for your mother since the first humans were born. They have scoured the earth waiting for the

Chosen One, yet it was you who showed me the way. Just as you helped me destroy Agartha"—he spread his arms wide—"all of this is because of you."

Jack shook his head as fresh tears sprang to his eyes.

"When you jumped from the bridge in Agartha, did you truly think I could not follow?" This time the smile did reach his eyes. "You led me here, boy. You have already joined me!"

Could it be true? Was it all because of him? Jack felt something solid against his back. Though he hadn't realized he was moving, he had backed up against the wall of the blacksmith's shop. As he stared up at the Assassin, a small movement caught Jack's eye. Limping out of the forest behind the Assassin was Killer, the second circus lion.

"I'm not going to hurt you, boy. I am here to show you the way."

Jack crumbled to his knees at the feet of the Assassin, far too exhausted to fight any longer.

"'And the child will bow before the Assassin,'" the Assassin whispered. "'And the child shall destroy the Awakened.' You have fulfilled the first part of the prophecy." The Assassin extended his hand as he spoke. "Now, rise and join me in fulfilling the second half. Help me destroy the Awakened once and for all." His icy blue eyes shifted into endless caverns of fire. "Together we will rule this world!"

With a snarl, Killer bolted forward and pounced, yet the Assassin moved like lightning. Spinning around, he grabbed the lion by the neck. He snarled at Killer and hurled the lion away. Killer whimpered as he slammed into a nearby wall and dropped to the ground.

As the Assassin turned to face Jack, the black sword slid deep into the Assassin's belly. Jack stood before him with both hands clasping the hilt.

The Assassin's eyes went wide with shock. As he stepped back, Ashandar slipped from his belly, leaving the sword in Jack's hands. The Assassin pressed his hands tight against his stomach as dark wind exploded from the gaping wound. Ten thousand voices exploded from the Shadowfog, shrieking in horror.

"This isn't over!" he screamed. Black blood leaked from between his fingers, and where it landed, it seared the ground. "This is far from over!" With a final snarl, the boiling Shadowfog whipped around him like a whirlwind, and a moment later, both the Assassin and the Shadowfog were gone.

Jack stumbled over to Killer who lay unmoving on the ground. The lion looked at Jack and let out a quiet sigh as the light left its eyes. Something cold had formed inside Jack's chest, choking all warmth from his body. This was the second time a lion had died to save him. And as he stood, Jack felt empty inside. He threw his head back and howled. Elion had told him something terrible would happen if he came back, but he hadn't listened. With tears in his eyes, he struggled to his feet, turning to look at the burning buildings.

All of it was because of him. He looked down the path leading toward his house. He knew it was hopeless, but he had to see. In his heart he still held to one last, desperate hope. Maybe his mother was still alive. With Ashandar in hand, Jack ran.

As he arrived at the edge of the woods outside his house, he stopped. There, in the front yard, was his mother lying flat on her back. Jack could see himself, the Jack from the past, lying unconscious on top of her. Sitting beside her body was Alexia, and standing over her was Mrs. Dumphry.

Jack circled around, being careful not to be seen. As four Oriax burst from the woods, Alexia picked up the Jack from the past, placed him on her back, and ran toward the house.

Off to Jack's left, Wild sprinted past. Wild was so intent on the rushing Oriax that he didn't see Jack. A moment later Arthur stumbled into the scene. He had a cloth wrapped around his head, pulled low over his eyes.

Jack crumbled to his knees as all hope left him. Through teary eyes he saw Wild loose his arrows at the Oriax and Alexia dive to the ground. Mrs. Dumphry sent streams of fire into two of the beasts, burning them to a crisp. And somewhere far in the distance, Jack heard the ring of Time. A moment before he felt himself flying backward through the air, Jack had one, final thought. *I must warn myself not to come back here!*

Chapter 25

AN ENDING TO REMEMBER

Jack opened his eyes to the ringing of bells. He was lying on the forest floor, feeling hollow inside. He tried to remember what he had just been doing, but nothing came. As he sat up, he saw himself sprinting through the woods with the Shadowfog pursuing close behind. The Jack from the past wasn't watching where he was running, but had turned to look behind him. Jack barely had time to think before the fleeing Jack tripped over him and landed flat on his face.

A moment later the Shadowfog flowed over both Jacks like a mighty ocean. Jack's mind cleared as he crawled arm over arm, making his way to himself. The black sword was still in his hands and was the only thing keeping the Shadowfog from touching either of the two Jacks.

As he crawled, Jack wept uncontrollably, unable to find a coherent thought. Yet he must warn himself. He knew he had to say something! Reaching out, he grabbed the other Jack's shoulder. The Jack from the past cried out in fear as he turned to look at him.

"You have to listen to them, do you hear me?" Jack screamed. "You have to listen! It's you who kills them! You kill them all, don't you understand? Mother, the town, Agartha! It's all your fault!" Even as he said the words, he knew they were wrong. He knew the other Jack wouldn't understand them. But he couldn't think straight.

He rolled on top of himself. The only thought in his head was that if he killed the Jack from the past, maybe he could stop it all. The other Jack wrestled with him, trying to keep his hands from choking him as the Shadowfog crashed over them, whipping earth and branches into the air. As Jack choked himself, the other Jack's eyes began to roll back. And then he heard it, the ring of Time.

"No!" he screamed through blinding tears.

And once again Jack was flying backward through the air.

When Jack returned to Agartha, it was a city in ruins. Collapsed bridges, pulverized chambers, and diluted streams were all that was left of the once-grand city. While he walked through the destruction, he passed many of the Awakened who'd lived through the battle, but he barely saw them. Jack felt more lost than ever before.

When Arthur spotted his best friend stumbling aimlessly, he ran over and wrapped Jack in a fierce hug. But Jack didn't hug him back; he couldn't. Arthur's head was bandaged, his arm wrapped in a sling. How could he hug his friend? It had been Jack who led the Assassin to Agartha and to Ballylesson. For all Jack knew, Arthur's parents might have died in the attack.

"Everyone thought you were dead!" Arthur cried as he hugged his friend yet again. "Andreal said you'd left the Awakened and joined the Assassin. But I told him he was wrong! Giant or not, no one is going to accuse my best friend of such a thing! I knew you were alive; I knew you wouldn't leave us!"

Jack didn't know what to say. He had left them. He had failed his friends.

"Where have you been? We've been searching for you for hours now." Arthur was both excited and concerned. "Are you hurt?"

"No," Jack said numbly.

"Well, you don't look right." Arthur grabbed Jack's arm. "Come with me. I need to take you to the Council. Everyone's been looking for you! And if you're hurt, they'll know what to do."

Jack let Arthur lead him through the rubble.

"I don't know about you," Arthur continued, "but I missed the entire battle." He threw his arms in the air. "After you didn't jump—what were you thinking by the way? The jump wasn't that far. Anyway, just after we landed, Alexia ran off acting all crazy. She killed a Shadule, Jack! Can you believe it?" His voice was filled with wonder. "The only other person to ever kill a Shadule was Mrs. Dumphry—at least that's what I've heard."

Arthur was becoming more animated by the second. "I don't know how she did it—Alexia, I mean, although I guess I don't know how Mrs. Dumphry did it either—but, when they found Alexia, she was lying on top of the Shadule, and it was as flat as a pancake. She won't tell me what happened. Maybe she doesn't remember. I don't know, but I spent the entire battle locked in one of the lower chambers. Wild just threw me in and left me there!"

Jack was barely listening. He no longer had the energy to care about any of it. Nothing mattered anymore. Arthur led him toward the Council Chamber, talking continuously, telling Jack of the little he'd seen or heard of the battle. After more than an hour of walking, they ran into Alexia who was walking stiffly with Wild at her side. Wild had a black eye and a few cuts on his face, but otherwise seemed okay. As they walked, he was trying to help Alexia, but she kept pushing him away irritably.

When she saw Jack, Alexia smiled and wrapped him in a hug. "I knew you were all right," she whispered. But Jack just stared at the ground, unable to meet her eyes. Without a word, she and Wild turned and joined Jack and Arthur on their walk to the Council Chamber.

"They found Mrs. Dumphry on a bridge far below," Arthur continued. "She must have fallen or something. But she's alive, although she's in a terrible mood and has been snapping at everyone."

At least I didn't kill her too. There's one thing that's not my fault, Jack thought glumly.

When he refused to respond, Arthur finally quieted. As they walked, Jack began noticing the citizens of Agartha. Everyone he saw had an injury of some kind. Heads, ribs, arms, and legs were bandaged. And everyone they passed stopped to stare. There were some who stared at Jack and his friends with wonder, yet most also had fear in their eyes.

As they passed a group of men and women standing on a small bridge, Alexia snarled, "What are you looking at? Get out of here!" All of the adults quickly turned and ran. Alexia gave Jack an embarrassed look. "It's only gotten worse since the battle. They're afraid of us, Jack. Even the Council seems afraid."

"They should be," Jack said bitterly. "The city was destroyed because of me. I am the one who will destroy them. They should run as far from me as possible."

Everyone went silent at this. Although they should have been able to arrive at the Council Chamber rather quickly, they kept finding bridges that had been destroyed. Each time they came to one of these, they had to search for another way.

Throughout the city, many of the bridges and chambers were gone, yet somehow, impossibly, the city hadn't collapsed. In some places, half a bridge had gone missing, though the other half stayed standing. A chamber supporting six bridges was completely destroyed, yet the bridges stood strong. It didn't make sense, but Jack was far too exhausted to spend a moment thinking about it.

An hour and seven minutes later, Jack, Arthur, Alexia, and Wild walked across the half-crumbled bridge to the Council Chamber. As they arrived, Jack noticed that all the tapestries and the massive structure of interlocking silvery rings had been completely destroyed. Only five of the Council members were present.

Mrs. Dumphry was the first to see the children. When her eyes fell on Jack, she clasped her hands together and sighed. "The Author be praised," she said. At the same moment, Elion murmured, "Jack Staples lives."

There was no wall or door to speak of, so Jack and the others simply walked over the ruined entry and into the chamber. Aias was there, though his left arm now ended at his elbow. The fire-haired giant, Andreal, was also there and had a large bandage wrapping his ribs. Miel knelt by his side, her hands moving in a strange pattern over a deep gash in the giant's leg, and as she moved, the gash began to mend itself.

When the children reached the center of the chamber, Elion walked to Jack and wrapped her arms around him. Her eyes glowed, shifting colors constantly as she spoke. "It is good to see you, Jack. I prayed the Author would keep you safe, but I must admit, I was beginning to fear the worst."

Jack didn't hug her back, and he didn't cry. He just stepped back and spoke numbly, "He was right." Jack glanced at the giant. "You should have let him kill me. All of this was my fault."

Elion smiled sadly as she looked at Jack. "Sit down and tell us what happened."

Jack told them everything. He didn't care anymore. He didn't hold anything back. He told them about his mother, the town, the Shadule, and the Assassin—all of it. When he finished the horrific story, for a moment, no one said a word. They all just watched him with wide eyes.

Jack could feel the accusations in their stares. He knew what they were thinking: *It's you; you are the child who will destroy us!* Too exhausted and numb to think straight, he waited. He was sure any minute now one of them would pick him up and throw him off the edge of the ruined chamber.

When Elion spoke, she sounded thoughtful. "There is a reason the Assassin is also known as the Destroyer of Hope. There is a reason we call him the Father of Lies. You need to think, Jack. I know you are tired, but you must hear me. The Assassin has arranged things to make you believe this was your fault. He is the Deceiver, and the moment you choose to believe him, you are lost."

Jack couldn't meet her piercing eyes.

"You did not lead him to Ballylesson. He must have found it before you took him there, otherwise your journey never would have begun. The Father of Lies could only arrange things to happen the way they did because he had already discovered it. He may have found it after the circus fire or some other way. We may never know how, but hear me, none of this was your fault."

After a moment, Jack looked at her. Elion's eyes were fifty colors at the same time.

"Every choice you made was to try to save those you loved, and that is a noble thing. Your only mistake was to give yourself to your anger. Although it is right to fight evil, we must never fight evil with evil. Even in the fiercest of battles, your heart must stay pure, and your love must not waver. You will learn that love has a far sharper blade than rage." Her eyes shifted to Alexia. "This is a lesson you both must learn."

Alexia wiped a tear from her eye, though she nodded at Elion's words.

"The Deceiver has spun his webs with the hope of causing us to fight among ourselves. It is his desire that some might be ignorant enough to blame you, Jack." As she said this, she met Andreal's eyes. "Yet evil only has the power that we allow it, and we will not give the Assassin this power over us."

Aias stood slowly, and when he spoke, he sounded lost. "So what now? Where do we go, and how do we fight? It's not just the city we've lost, but many of the Awakened."

Elion was measured in her response. "This war began long before Time was born, but on the day of her birth, the war was brought into this world, and here it has stayed." She turned to look at Aias and the rest of the Council. "What now, you ask? We must end it. We don't have time to rebuild, and there is no stopping what's coming. We must take the journey and meet with Time. We need her wisdom now more than ever." Elion smiled as she turned to Jack and Alexia. "I think she will be very excited to meet you both."

Elion turned back to Aias. "Have courage, Aias! You have been on this earth far too long to let the loss of a city make you lose hope. And though we mourn those who have fallen, we also have reason to celebrate. Not only did Jack and Alexia both kill a Shadule, but Jack has done the unimaginable. He has wounded the Assassin himself! We are at war, and it is inevitable that cities will fall and many will die. And before this war is over, the darkness will grow far stronger, but these children have accomplished more for the Awakened in this one battle than any have accomplished in thousands of years. We're not the only ones who are hurting. Even as we sit here, the Assassin hides in the shadows like a wounded dog. And though we have lost much, thanks to Jack and Alexia, so has he."

Elion's eyes gathered even more light as she placed a comforting hand on Jack's shoulder. "We must find an Oasis for the Awakened to heal and continue their training, and we must gather the Lambs who are newly awakening. This battle was nothing compared to the storm that's coming. And we must take the Children of Prophecy to the Forbidden Garden where they will meet with Time."

Every eye turned to Jack and Alexia. Jack was so tired he could barely stand. All he wanted was to lie down and sleep for a year. Yet he had the sinking feeling that his journey was far from over.

Read on for an exciting excerpt from the next book in this series,
Jack Staples and the City of Shadows.

"It would be far easier to train an elephant to fly than to teach the heart," Mrs. Dumphry said, chuckling. "Can you imagine that?" She let out a great guffaw of laughter. "An elephant, flying! What a magnificent sight that would be. I wonder if any elephants have ever—" Mrs. Dumphry stopped. "What was I saying? Ah, that's right, you cannot instruct the heart. It must be awakened through experience. Just because you are one of the Awakened does not mean you are living fully awake …"

Jack Staples wasn't really listening to his ancient teacher; his eyes were glued to the sheer drop behind her. Mrs. Dumphry paced along the edge of a cliff without noticing when a toe or ankle hovered over empty space.

Alexia Dreager was standing beside him, and he could tell she was furious. Jack hoped she wasn't going to start yelling at Mrs. Dumphry again; it never ended well when she did.

Arthur Greaves stood next to Alexia and was obviously afraid; he'd turned at least four shades of green in the last thirty seconds. Arthur was Jack's closest friend, and Jack knew Arthur wasn't afraid of heights. It was the water far below that made him nervous. Arthur could barely swim a stroke.

Jack was getting a sinking feeling in the pit of his stomach. The past month had been filled with all sorts of crazy experiences. Mrs. Dumphry kept them busy doing some of the most ridiculous things Jack could never have imagined.

They'd spent every day in "School for the Awakened," as Mrs. Dumphry called it. However, very little of what they did was like any school Jack had heard of. Mrs. Dumphry had them eating strange food, reading poetry, singing songs, and learning language and dance. They'd spent a day climbing, another learning to juggle, and another cooking. They spent hours every day training with weapons and musical instruments.

Jack mostly trained with his black sword, Ashandar. Elion had told Jack it wasn't just a sword. It was also a teacher. The Sephari said it once belonged to the greatest Blades Master on earth, and if he could learn to surrender to it, Jack might also become great. Back in Ballylesson, he'd felt Ashandar's power when he fought Oriax and killed a Shadule. The blade had been alive in his hands. Yet no matter how often he practiced with the thing, he'd never been able to repeat what happened.

Jack felt his chest tighten. That had been the day his mother died. He'd tried to save her and instead had gotten her killed. Jack shuddered. He could picture her lying in a sea of green grass. The Assassin had killed his mother, and Jack had been too weak to stop him.

Jack enjoyed learning the sword because he knew he would need it if he were going to kill the Assassin. But the rest of it was infuriating. Every time he asked why they were learning such ridiculous things such as juggling or dance, Mrs. Dumphry would say something like, "Your imagination is a far more powerful weapon than a sword could ever be. If you learn the sword but have no imagination, your answer to every problem will be the sword."

Normally, Jack would have thought the whole thing a grand adventure. But his mother was dead and the city of Agartha had been destroyed. No matter what anyone said, he knew these things were at least partly his fault. To make matters worse, Jack's father and brother were missing, and he had no idea how to find them. Instead of searching for them or going back to bury his mother, or going anywhere at all for that matter, Jack and the others had been forced to wait in a small cabin somewhere outside of London. They'd arrived by boat a month earlier and had been waiting there ever since.

Mrs. Dumphry would tell them only that they were awaiting word from Elion that it was safe to leave Great Britain. When they asked where they were going, she claimed not to know. Jack hated doing nothing. He was sure the Assassin wasn't sitting around playing childish games.

I could time travel . . . He immediately dismissed the thought. *No. I won't do it again. Not if I can help it.* Jack had walked through time, though he wasn't sure he'd be able to do it again, even if he wanted to. He'd gone back to save his mother's life. But not only had he been unable to save her, but he'd hurt many others in the process.

Jack snapped back to attention. Mrs. Dumphry was standing with her back to the cliff and both heels hovering over empty space. A spattering of snow covered much of the ground, but Jack's shiver had nothing to do with the cold.

"What?" Arthur said, moaning.

"I said, I am going to count to three, then we will all jump together," Mrs. Dumphry repeated.

Jack struggled to catch his breath as his stomach churned. The cliff was impossibly high!

"I-I can't do it," Arthur stammered. "I'm not … I can't … the thing is, I'm not a good swimmer!" His eyes were wide. "I don't think I …"

"One!" Mrs. Dumphry's voice was a whip crack.

Arthur began talking faster. "It's just that I've never lived near water so I've only swam a couple times, and I …"

"Mrs. Dumphry, I really don't think this is safe!" Jack added.

"Two!"

Arthur's hand shot to his mouth as he turned and promptly vomited his breakfast on a nearby rock.

"Isn't the water going to be freezing? I think Arthur is right. It's probably best that we come back another time," Jack said hastily.

"Three!"

Without another word, Mrs. Dumphry leapt from the edge and folded her body into a cannonball position. When she hit the water far below, the splash shot high into the air.

Alexia grimaced at Jack, then rolled her eyes at Arthur. "You really need to stop doing that. You're worse than a little girl." Without so much as glancing down, she dove from the edge, keeping her body perfectly straight with toes pointed. When she entered the water, there was almost no splash at all.

Far below, Mrs. Dumphry surfaced, cackling loudly. A moment later she looked up in confusion. "A rabbit with the heart of a lion is far more powerful than a wolf that believes itself a mouse." Beside her, Alexia bobbed up, looking pleased.

Jack thought he was going to hyperventilate. He knew they had to jump; Mrs. Dumphry would stay down there all day, if she had to.

He glanced at Arthur and whispered, "It's going to be okay. She won't let you drown. Besides, if we wait, it will only make it worse, right?"

Jack closed his eyes and inhaled deeply. Screaming like a wild man, he ran off the top of the cliff. The fall lasted six and a half seconds, and as he surfaced, he gasped at the intensely cold water. Even still, he couldn't suppress a laugh. The fall had been exhilarating.

"Young Mr. Greaves," Mrs. Dumphry called, "my patience is wearing thin. You will jump now or I will throw you off."

"Come on, Arthur," Jack yelled. "It's really fun!"

Arthur took a step back, disappearing from view. "I can't do it!" he shouted.

Mrs. Dumphry *tsk*ed irritably, and a moment later, Jack heard a squeal from the top of the cliff. As he looked up, Arthur appeared. He was floating in midair and screaming hysterically as he hovered over the edge. Mrs. Dumphry watched with a look of concentration.

Arthur kicked his legs hysterically, flailing against something unseen. A moment later he shrieked as he dropped like a stone. A split second before he hit the water, twenty bolts of lightning streaked the sky.

Terror formed in the pit of Jack's stomach. Rocks and earth rained down as he tried to look in every direction at the same time. Mrs. Dumphry offered Jack an amused smile, then turned back to Arthur.

Ten, twenty, thirty bolts lit up the sky, striking the lake or the nearby land. With each bolt that struck the lake, Jack felt as if he'd been kicked in the ribs. "We're under attack!" he yelled. "The Assassin is here!"

A short distance away, Arthur surfaced, flailing wildly. "Help me!" he screamed.

"Arthur Reginald Greaves"—Mrs. Dumphry's voice was both commanding and reassuring—"you are safe! Face your fear, child. I will not let you drown."

Lightning struck just above Mrs. Dumphry's head, yet the bolt didn't hit her. Instead it slammed against a shield of blue light.

"Help!" Arthur wailed.

"Fear is not real, boy." Mrs. Dumphry treaded water calmly. "It is a locked door. Face it and you will find the key."

Arthur barely kept his head above water as lightning rained down.

"We need to run!" Jack screamed. "The Assassin has come!"

"Arthur, you can do this!" Mrs. Dumphry's voice held a note of authority that cut through the chaos. "Look at me." Arthur locked eyes with her. "Child, you are courageous, you are strong, and you are able. And it is you who controls the lightning."